讀李家同學英文 6

李家同◎著

Nick Hawkins（郝凱揚）◎翻譯

周正一・Nick Hawkins（郝凱揚）◎解析

Plum Blossom Village
李花村

透過李家同簡潔而寓意深遠的文章，領略用英文表達中文故事的妙趣

遠方的孩子◎李花村◎飆車◎深河

瓷娃娃◎我是我

序

李家同

　　我真該謝謝郝凱揚先生將我的文章譯成了英文。這當然不是一件簡單的事情，但是我看了他的翻譯，我發現他的翻譯是絕對正確的，而且非常優美。外國人寫的小說，往往用字非常艱難。對一般人而言，都太難了。這本書比較容易，沒有用太難的字。郝先生是美國人，能做這件事情，充分展現他的中英文造詣很高，他一定是一位非常聰明的人。

　　這一本書最大的好處是有對英文的註解、也有練習，想學英文的年輕人可以從註解中學到很多英文的基本學問。

　　我在此給讀者一個建議：你不妨先看看中文文章，先不看英文的翻譯，然後試著將中文翻成英文，我相信你一定會覺得中翻英好困難。譯完以後，再去看郝先生的翻譯，相信你可以學到不少，也可以寫出越來越像外國人寫的句子。

　　我尤其希望讀者注意標點符號的用法。英文的標點符號是非常重要的，中文句子對標點符號的標準比較寬鬆，但英文絕對不行，一個標點符號用錯了，全句的結構就是錯了。讀者可以利用這個機會好好

地學會如何正確地下英文的標點符號。

另外，千萬要注意動詞的用法，如果你英文動詞沒有錯，你的英文就很厲害了。信不信由你，英文不好的人常常不會用現在完成式，可是這本書裡用了很多的現在完成式，你不妨仔細研究為什麼要用這種我們中國人所不熟悉的時態。

在英文句子裡，一定要有一個主詞和一個動詞，讀者不妨在每一個句子裡去找一下，主詞和動詞一定會存在。我們中國人有時寫一個英文句子，但是句子中，主詞和動詞弄不清楚，以至於有的動詞沒有主詞。也就因為如此，凡是這種主詞和動詞關係不清楚的句子，意思也會弄不清楚。讀者如果覺得這些文章很容易懂，其實完全是因為每一個句子的主詞和動詞都很清楚的原因。

如果你有時不知道如何用英文表達你的想法，你應該知道，這是正常的事。多看這本書，對你一定有幫助。

看這本書的時候，再次建議你先看中文，立刻試譯，再參考英譯。這樣做，對你的英文作文會有很大的好處。

最後我謝謝周先生，他的註解使這本書生色不少。當然我也該謝謝聯經出版公司，我相信這本書的出版會有助於很多想學好英文的年輕人，這本書能夠順利出現，林載爵先生和何采嬪女士有很大的功勞，我在此謝謝他們。

起而行

郝凱揚

李家同令人敬佩的地方，不在於他淵博的學問，也不在於他虔誠的信仰。我之所以佩服他，是因為他將他的理想付諸行動。

眾人皆知，李教授信奉的是天主教，而且他以他的信仰為寫作的出發點。在台灣，即使把天主教、基督教和摩門教三大派基督徒的人數全部加起來，所佔的比例還不到人口的一成。那麼，一個天主教徒寫的書怎麼會在台灣的社會廣受歡迎呢？關鍵在於「付諸行動」四個字。

幾年前，我在台灣當過兩年的傳教士。當我問人家「你有什麼宗教信仰」時，最常聽到的一句話是「所有的宗教都是勸人為善」。其實我並非不知道，說這句話的用意是以較為委婉的口氣拒絕我，但這十一個字所蘊含的意義非常深遠。儒家的「仁義」、道家的「道」、佛教的「慈悲」、基督徒的「博愛」、甚至無神論的「倫理」，宗旨都不外乎教人把內在的善性發揮出來。然而光說好聽的話沒有用——真正的信徒一定要實踐他的信仰，否則他只是個偽善者。李家同主要不是個作者，乃是個「做者」：文作得少，事做得多。也就是因為如此，才有這麼多的讀者閱讀他的書，並從中得到感動。

「實踐」是個極為管用的通則，我們不妨想想它如何適用在語言的學習上。假如一個人(我們不說他是誰)訂了一年的美語雜誌，每個月固定讀一本上好的英文教材，但他從來不寫半個英文字，也不說半句英語，試問，他的英文能力會突飛猛進嗎？他對自己的英文能力會有很大的信心嗎？我再來做另一個假設：倘若另一個人(我們依然不說他是誰)買不起最好的英文教材，但他喜歡跟幾個不會中文的外國朋友見面，也喜歡寫英文日記或部落格，那麼英文會不會豐富他的人生？他會不會比較容易記住他所學的東西？

你自己比較像這兩個人中的哪一個？如果你的答案令你不滿，你要如何改變你學英文的方式？以我學中文的經驗來說，我覺得最重要的是給自己一個愛學的理由和非練習不可的環境。愛學的理由可以好玩(想唱美國的流行音樂)；文雅(更能欣賞英國文學)；不良(可以搭訕外國女生)；實際(要跟國外的客戶做生意)；無聊(愛挑布希總統的語病)等等，找出自己的理由應該不難。尋找非練習不可的環境對無法長期出國的人可能沒那麼容易，可是並非不可能——除了以上提過的，和不會中文的外國人交朋友以及利用網路寫英文部落格，還有別的方法。還有，在學會講英文的過程中，一定要多出一些難堪的錯，發現了之後笑一笑自己，因為這樣才算豁了出去。如果你因為怕出糗而只講最簡單的英文，怎麼會進步？你又不是沒聽過四聲不準的外國學生說「我恨矮台灣人」(我很愛台灣人)啦！

最後我想說，我絕對不是個隨隨便便的譯者和解析者——把這些精采的故事譯成傳神的英文花了我不少心思。目的只有一個——希望你能藉此體會到學英文的樂趣！至於進步，我和解析者周正一先生只能提供好的資源——要不要好好利用，完全由你決定了。

編學相長

周正一

「讀李家同學英文」系列邁入第六輯了，這真是不得了的成就。參與其中的編寫，當然與有榮焉。

首先要承認，在進行句型和重點的解析過程中，時時會碰到瓶頸。在把原作和譯文讀過之後，我會開始尋找各級程度的讀者必須要了解的重點，之後開始絞盡腦汁，尋思怎麼進行解析說明，幫助讀者在看過解析之後，能留下鮮明且久遠的記憶。

其實英文的固定句型畢竟有限，從第一輯到第五輯一路讀來的讀者應會發現，有些句型重複出現了。但是這裡要強調的是，即使句型相同，英文的寫法仍有多種變化，解說的角度和方式也會有所不同。

另外，在編寫時，我並不刻意強調著重文法，以免產生不必要的畏懼感和排斥感。但對學習英文至關緊要，比如假設語氣，那當然無法避免。我會盡力根據多年教學英文的經驗，輔以實例解說，以期解惑。片(成)語反倒較令我頭痛，因為它就和生字一樣，沒啥道理可言。讓學習英語的人，尤其是初學者非常頭痛。

　　再者，在解析完每個重點後，無論是句型、文法或片語，我都會附上用心設計的小試身手，讓讀者在實作中進一步去體會驗證。

　　這是一本三合一的學習書，就原作來說，我們可以欣賞到李家同充滿人性關懷和無限想像的文章。流暢的譯文和每書所附的譯文朗讀 CD 可以把讀者的英文程度提升到一個更高的層次。至於我所負責的解析，則是輔助句型片語或文法這些工具，期望讀者對作者譯者的文字有更深刻的了解。

　　欲學習英文有成，興趣是不可少的動力來源。打開這一系列的任何一輯，去欣賞它、了解它、學習它，一定會有意想不到的進步。有句話說，教學相長。然而從參與編寫的過程中，我體悟到一個心得，亦即：豈只教學相長？從編寫中，我也學到許多──從故事中，學到開闊恢宏，光明清滌的人性；從譯文中，我更學到不少前所未知的英文。學無止境，凡用心走過的，都是成長，都是收穫。

　　最後用以下這句話和讀者共勉開卷有益。

A book well written is something more than a collection of hundreds of printed pages. It is a wealth of wisdom and a well of pleasure.

目次
CONTENTS

Plum Blossom Village
李花村

1-5

當時只記入山深，

青溪幾曲到雲林；

春來遍是桃花水，

不辨仙源何處尋。

──王維《桃源行》

　　孩子送來的時候，看上去還不太嚴重，可是當時我就感到有些不妙，根據我在竹東榮民醫院服務三十多年的經驗，這孩子可能得了川崎症，這種病只有小孩子會得，相當危險的。我告訴孩子父母，孩子必須住院，他們有點困惑，因為小孩子看上去精神還滿好的，甚至不時做些胡鬧的舉動，不過他們很合作，一切聽我的安排。

　　我一方面請護理人員做了很多必要的檢查，一方面將其他幾位對川崎症有經驗的醫生都找來了，我們看了實驗室送來的報告，發現孩子果真得了川崎症，而且是高度危險的一種，可能活不過今晚了。

CD1-2

◇ (標題)blossom (n.)(果樹的)花
◇ winding (adj.) 蜿蜒的
◇ misty (adj.) 朦朧多霧的
◇ strew (v.) 撒；散落 (不規則過去分詞為strewn)
◇ fountainhead (n.) 源頭
◇ immortal (n.) 神仙；不朽人物

◇ veteran (n.)退役軍人 (veterans' hospital為「榮民醫院」)
◇ severe (adj.) 嚴重的
◇ pediatric (adj.) 小兒科的(pediatrics為「小兒科」)
◇ bewildered (adj.) 困惑的
◇ mischief (n.) 惡作劇

He only remembers it was somewhere deep in the mountains,

Up a winding blue stream, in a misty forest.

Now spring has come, and the water is strewn with peach blossoms,

But the fountainhead of the immortals is nowhere to be found.

- Wang Wei, "Journey to Peach Blossom Fountainhead"

When they brought the boy in, it didn't look too serious, but I had a bad feeling nonetheless. Based on my thirty-plus years of experience working at the Zhudong Veterans' Hospital, I thought he might have Kawasaki disease, a severe pediatric illness. When I told the boy's parents that he needed to spend the night in the hospital, they were a bit bewildered, as by all appearances their son looked like he was feeling fine—he even made a little mischief here and there. But they were very cooperative and accepted all my recommendations.

Once I'd asked the nursing staff to carry out various necessary tests, I called together the few other doctors who had experience dealing with Kawasaki disease. We took a look at the lab test results and found that sure enough, the boy had the disease—in fact, he had a particularly dangerous form of it, and he might not live through the night.

◇ recommendation (n.) 推薦；建議
◇ staff (n.) (全體)職員
◇ various (adj.) 許多的；各式各樣的
◇ deal with (v.) 處理；對付

◇ lab (n.) 實驗室 (laboratory 的縮寫)
◇ sure enough (adv.) 果然
◇ particularly (adv.) 特別地；格外

　　到了晚上十點鐘，距離孩子住進醫院只有五個小時，孩子的情況急轉直下，到了十點半，孩子竟然昏迷不醒了，我只好將實情告訴了孩子的父母，他們第一次聽到川崎症，當我婉轉地告訴他們，孩子可能過不了今天晚上以後，孩子的媽媽立刻昏了過去，他的爸爸丟開了孩子，慌作一團地去救孩子的媽媽，全家陷入一片愁雲慘霧之中。也難怪，這個小孩好可愛，一副聰明相，只有六歲，是這對夫婦唯一的孩子。

　　孩子的祖父也來了，已經七十五歲，身體健朗得很，他是全家最鎮靜的一位，不時安慰兒子和媳婦，他告訴我，孩子和他幾乎相依為命，因為爸爸媽媽都要上班，孩子和爺爺奶奶相處的時間很長。

6-10　　孩子的祖父一再地說：「我已經七十五歲，我可以走了，偏偏身體好好的，孩子這麼小，為什麼不能多活幾年？」

　　我行醫已經快四十年了，以目前情況來看，我相信孩子存活的機會非常小，可是我仍安排他住進加護病房，孩子臉上罩上了氧氣罩，靜靜地躺著。我忽然跪下來作了一個非常誠懇的祈禱，我向上蒼說，我

◇ dramatic (adj.) 戲劇化的
◇ delicately (adv.) 婉轉地
◇ faint (v.) 昏倒
◇ panicked (adj.) 恐慌的

◇ gloom (n.) 陰暗
◇ sprightly (adj.) 生氣勃勃的（注意：雖然字尾是ly，但仍為形容詞）
◇ self-possessed (adj.) 鎮定的

At 10 pm, five hours after the boy had arrived at the hospital, he took a dramatic turn for the worse. At 10:30, he actually slipped into a coma. I was forced to explain the situation to his parents, who had never heard of Kawasaki disease. When I delicately told them that their boy might not make it through the night, the mother fainted on the spot, and the panicked father temporarily forgot his son as he rushed to come to his wife's aid. A dark cloud of gloom descended on the entire family. It wasn't hard to see why—he was a beautiful boy, very intelligent-looking, only six years old, and he was the couple's only child.

The boy's grandfather, a sprightly old man of 75, had also come to the hospital. The most self-possessed of the family, he comforted his son and his daughter-in-law as best he could. He told me that he and the boy virtually lived for each other. Because the boy's parents both worked, he and his grandson spent a great deal of time together.

The grandfather kept saying, "I'm seventy-five years old—why 6-10
am I the healthy one? Why can't such a little boy live for a few more years?"

I've been a doctor for nearly forty years; judging by the look of things, I knew that the boy's chances of survival were very slim. In spite of that, however, I had him put in the ICU. He lay there quietly, an oxygen mask covering his face. Suddenly I knelt down and said

---

◇ survival (n.) 倖存
◇ slim (adj.)(指希望、機會)渺茫的
　　(slim的原意為「苗條的」)

◇ oxygen (n.)氧氣
◇ kneel (v.) 跪下 (不規則過去分詞為
　　knelt)

願意走，希望上蒼將孩子留下來。理由很簡單，我已六十五歲，這一輩子活得豐富而舒適，我已對人世沒什麼眷戀，可是孩子只有六歲，讓他活下去，好好地享受人生吧！

　　孩子的情況雖然穩定了下來，但也沒有改善，清晨六時，接替我的王醫生來了，他看我一臉的倦容，勸我趕快回家睡覺。

　　我發動車子以後，忽然想到鄉下去透透氣，於是沿著路向五指山開去，這條路風景奇佳，清晨更美。

　　忽然我看到了一個往李花村的牌子，我這條路已經走過了幾十次，從來不知道有叫李花村的地方，可是不久我又看到往李花村的牌子，大概二十分鐘以後，我發現一條往右轉的路，李花村到了。到李花村不能開車進去，只有一條可以步行或騎腳踏車的便道。

11-15　　走了十分鐘，李花村的美景在我面前一覽無遺，李花村是一個山谷，山谷裡漫山遍野地種滿李花，當時正是二月，白色的李花像白雲

◇ earnest (adv.) 誠懇的
◇ stabilize (v.) 變穩定
◇ relieve (v.) 換……的班；接手……的工作
◇ exhausted (adv.) 筋疲力盡的
◇ heed (v.) 聽從
◇ stunning (adj.) 極漂亮的；令人目瞪口呆的

an unusually earnest prayer. "I'm willing to die, but I hope You will preserve this boy," I said to God. "The reason is simple: I'm 65 years old. I've lived a full and comfortable life; now I'm ready to take my leave of this world. But this boy is only six! Please let him live. Let him enjoy what life has to offer."

Remarkably, the boy's situation stabilized, but it still didn't improve. Then, at six in the morning, Doctor Wang came to relieve me. Seeing how exhausted I was, he urged me to go home and rest.

After I started my car, I felt a sudden desire to go someplace where I could get some fresh air. Heeding it, I headed toward Five Fingers Mountain. In the early morning, the beautiful scenery along the road looked particularly stunning.

All of a sudden I noticed a sign that said I was approaching Plum Blossom Village. Despite having driven that road twenty or thirty times before, I'd never noticed any place called Plum Blossom Village. But it wasn't long before I saw another sign for it. About twenty minutes later, there was a turnoff on the right: I had arrived. It was impossible to drive into the village—the only way in was via a path you could walk or bike down.

I had walked for scarcely ten minutes when the breathtaking sight of the village appeared before my eyes. It was a valley, virtually every square inch of which was planted with plum blossoms. On that

11-15

◇ approach (v.) 接近　　　　　◇ via (prep.) 經由
◇ turnoff (v.) 旁道；側路　　　◇ scarcely (adv.) 幾乎沒有，幾乎不

一般地將整個山谷蓋了起來。

　　可是，李花村給我最深刻的印象，卻不是白色的李花，而是李花村使我想起了四十年前台灣的鄉下：這裡看不到一輛汽車，除了走路以外，只能騎腳踏車。我也注意到那些農舍裡冒出的炊煙，顯然大家都用柴火燒早飯，更使我感到有趣的是一家雜貨店，一大清早，雜貨店就開門了，有人在買油，他帶了一只瓶子，店主用漏斗從一只大桶裡倒油給他，另一位客人要買兩塊豆腐乳，他帶了一只碗來，店主從一只缸裡小心翼翼地揀了兩塊豆腐乳，放在他的碗裡面。

　　我在街上漫無目的地亂逛，有一位中年人看到了我，他說：「張醫生早」，我問他怎麼知道我是張醫生，他指指我身上的名牌，我這才想起我沒脫下醫生的白袍子。

　　中年人說，「張醫生，看起來你似乎一晚上都沒睡覺，要不要到我家去休息一下？」我累得不得了，就答應了。中年人的家也使我想起了四十年前的台灣鄉下房子，他的媽媽問我要不要吃早飯，我當然答

◇ impression (n.) 印象
◇ rather (adv.) 倒是；反而是
◇ remind (v.) 使……(回)想到
◇ chimney (n.) 煙囪

◇ indicate (v.) 表示
◇ charming (adj.) 可愛；迷人的
◇ barrel (n.) 大桶
◇ funnel (n.) 漏斗

February day, the white blossoms covered the valley like clouds.

But it wasn't the white plum blossoms that made the greatest impression on me. Rather, it was how the village reminded me of the way the Taiwanese countryside used to look forty years ago. There was not a single car—besides walking, the only way to get around was by bicycle. I noticed the smoke coming from the farmhouse chimneys, which indicated that the villagers still used wood-burning stoves to cook. A grocery store, already open at that early hour, was even more charming. A customer was buying cooking oil; he had brought a bottle, which the storekeeper filled from a large barrel of oil using a funnel. Another customer wanted to buy two pieces of fermented tofu; he had brought a bowl, which the storekeeper filled with two pieces of fermented tofu carefully chosen from a vat.

As I wandered aimlessly through the streets, a middle-aged man noticed me. "Good morning, Doctor Zhang," he said. When I asked him how he knew my name, he pointed to the nametag on my chest. Only then did I realize that I'd forgotten to remove my white physician's coat.

"Doctor Zhang, you look like you haven't slept all night," the man said. "Would you like to come to my house for a nap?" Being exhausted, I told him I'd love to. Like the village, the man's house reminded me of the way rural Taiwanese houses looked forty years ago. His mother asked me if I'd like some breakfast; of course, I said

◇ fermented (adj.) 發酵的
◇ vat (n.) 缸；甕

◇ aimlessly (adv.) 漫無目的地

應，老太太在燒柴的爐子上熱了一鍋稀飯，煎了一只荷包蛋，還給了我一個熱饅頭，配上花生米和醬瓜，我吃得好舒服。

吃完早餐以後，我躺在竹床上睡著了，醒來，發現已經十二點，溫暖的陽光使我眼睛有點睜不開，看到李花村如此安詳、如此純樸，我實在很想留下來，可是又想起那得了川崎症的孩子。我看到一支電話，就問那位在廚房裡忙的老太太，可不可以借用他們的電話打到竹東去，因為我關心竹東榮民醫院的一位病人。老太太告訴我這支電話只能通到李花村，打不出去的，她說如果我記掛竹東的病人，就必須回去看。

16-20　　我謝謝老太太，請她轉告她的兒子，我要回去看我的病人了。沿著進來的路走出李花村，開車回到竹東榮民醫院，令我感到無限快樂的是，孩子活回來了，不但脫離了險境，而且三天以後，孩子就出院了。這真是奇蹟。

我呢？我一直想再回李花村看看。可是卻再也找不到李花村了，我一共試了五次，每次都看不到往李花村的牌子，那條往右轉的路也

◇ homey（adj.）像在自己家裡那樣親切、舒服的
◇ serene（adj.）平靜的；沒有煩惱的
◇ long（v.）渴望（多指得不到或做不到的事，後面接 to+V. 或 for+N.）
◇ concerned（adj.）擔心的

I would. The old woman heated up a pot of porridge on the stove, fried an egg sunny side up, and gave me a hot steamed bun with peanuts and pickled cucumbers. It was a wonderfully homey meal.

Once I finished eating, I lay down on a bamboo bed for a nap. By the time I woke up, it was noon, and the warm sunlight made it difficult for me to open my eyes. Seeing how simple and serene Plum Blossom Village was, I longed to stay there a while longer. But then my thoughts turned to the boy with Kawasaki disease. I noticed there was a phone in the house, and I asked the old woman, who was busy in the kitchen, if I could use it to make a call to Zhudong to check on a patient in the veterans' hospital there. "Our phone can only make calls within the village," she said. "If you're concerned about your patient, I'm afraid you'll have to go check on him in person."

I thanked the woman and asked her to tell her son that I'd gone back to check on my patient. I left the village the way I'd come in and drove back to the Zhudong Veterans' Hospital. To my immeasurable joy, I found that the boy had lived! Not only did he survive the crisis, but he left the hospital three days later. It was truly a miracle.

And me? I yearned to return to Plum Blossom Village for another visit, but no matter how hard I tried, I couldn't find it again. I tried a total of five times, but I never saw the signpost leading to the village, and the turnoff on the right had disappeared. All I saw on

16-20

⬦ immeasurable (adj.) 不可計量的　　⬦ signpost (n.) 路標
⬦ crisis (n.) 危機

不見了，在公路的右邊，只看到山和樹林。我根本不敢和任何人談起我的經驗，大家一定會認為我老糊塗了，竹東山裡哪有一個開滿了李花的地方？

　　這是半年前的事。昨天晚上我值班，急診室送來了一個小孩子，他爸爸騎機車載他，車子緊急煞車，孩子飛了出去，頭碰到地，沒有戴安全帽，其結果可想而知，他被送進醫院的時候，連耳朵裡都在不斷地流出血來。我們立刻將他送入手術室，打開他的頭蓋骨，發現他腦子裡已經充血，我們不但要吸掉腦子裡的血，還要替他取出腦袋裡折斷的骨頭，如果他能活下去，我們得替他裝一塊人工不鏽鋼的骨頭。

　　手術完，孩子的情況越來越危險，能恢復的機會幾乎小到零，可是我知道我如何可以救孩子的命，我跪下來向上蒼祈禱，「只要小孩子活下去，我可以走。」我是真心的，不是亂開支票。如果孩子活了，我知道我該到那裡去。

◇ slam（v.）猛踩；猛打；甩（常用於slam the door「猛地把門關上」，slam on the brakes「猛踩煞車」等片語）
◇ handlebars（n.）（機車或單車的）手把（多用複數）

◇ skull（n.）頭蓋骨
◇ cerebral（v.）（醫）腦部的
◇ hyperemia（n.）（醫）充血
◇ draw out（v.）汲出
◇ extract（v.）取出

the right side of the highway were mountains and trees. I didn't dare mention my experience to anyone for fear they'd think I was crazy— how could there possibly be a village planted full of flowers in the mountains of Zhudong?

Now six months have passed since my trip to Plum Blossom Village. Last night, while I was on duty, a boy was brought to the emergency room. His father had been taking him somewhere on his scooter when he was forced to slam on the brakes. The boy, who was not wearing a helmet, flew over the handlebars and hit his head on the ground. You can imagine the result without me having to describe it in detail—when the boy was brought in, even his ears were bleeding. We took him straight into the operating room, opened up his skull and found that he was experiencing cerebral hyperemia. Not only would we have to draw out the blood from his brain, we'd have to extract the broken bones there as well. If he lived, we would have to replace his bones with stainless steel.

We finished the procedure, but the boy's condition continued to deteriorate; his chance of recovery was virtually nil. Nevertheless, I knew there was a way to save him. I knelt down and prayed to God: "As long as this boy lives, I'm willing to die." And I meant it—I wasn't just blowing smoke. If the boy lived, I knew where I had to go.

◇ deteriorate (v.) 惡化
◇ nil (n.) 零

◇ blow smoke 亂說話

清晨五點，一位護士興奮地把我叫進加護病房，那個小孩子睜大眼睛，要喝楊桃汁。他也認得他的父母，他的爸爸抱著他大哭了起來，孩子有些不耐煩，用手推開爸爸，原來他手腳都能動了。

21-25 我們在早上八點，將孩子移出加護病房，孩子的爸爸拚命地謝我，他說他再也不敢騎機車載孩子了，又一再稱讚我醫術高明。

我當然知道這是怎麼一回事，我醫術再高明，也救不了這孩子的。

等到一切安置妥當以後，我回到了辦公室，寫了一封信給院長，一封給我的助理，將我的一件羽毛衣送給他，拜託他好好照顧窗口白色的非洲槿，同時勸他早日安定下來，找位賢妻良母型的女孩子結婚。

我上了車，向五指山開去，我知道，這次我一定會找到李花村。

果真，往李花村的牌子出現了。我將車子停好以後，輕快地走進了李花村，那位中年人又出現了，他說，「張醫生，歡迎你回來，這一

◇ embrace (v.) 擁抱（比hug更有感情）
◇ weep (v.) 哭泣（wept為不規則過去分詞）
◇ intensive care (n.) 加護病房（亦作 intensive care unit，簡稱 ICU）
◇ brilliant (adj.) 才華洋溢的
◇ the latter (n.) 後者（和 the former「前者」相對）

At 5 am, an excited-looking nurse called me into the ICU. The boy had opened his eyes wide and was asking for a drink of starfruit juice. Remarkably, he recognized his parents. His father embraced him and wept like a child. The boy pushed him away impatiently—apparently he was able to move his arms and legs.

At 8 am, we moved the boy out of intensive care. His father thanked me profusely and promised he would never take his son anywhere on a scooter again. He also kept saying what a brilliant doctor I was.

21-25

Of course, I knew that even if I was the most brilliant doctor in the world, I couldn't have saved the boy on my own.

Once I'd taken care of everything, I returned to my office. There, I wrote a letter to the hospital director and a letter to my assistant. I gave the latter my fur coat and asked him to take good care of the white African hibiscus in the window. I also urged him to settle down someday soon with a good, virtuous wife.

Then I got in my car and headed toward Five Fingers Mountain. This time, I knew that Plum Blossom Village would be there.

Sure enough, the signpost was there. I parked the car and walked toward the village with a quick step and a light heart. The same middle-aged man appeared to greet me. "Welcome back, Doctor

◇ settle down (v.) 安定下來 (這裡指成 家)　　◇ virtuous (adj.) 有道德的

次，你要留下來了吧？」我點點頭，這一次，我不會離開李花村了。

26-28　　附記：

　　《聯合報》竹苗版的新聞報導，竹東榮民醫院的張醫生去世了，張醫生在竹東醫院行醫三十年，他的忽然去世，令大家傷感不已，因為張醫生生前喜愛小朋友，常常陪病童玩耍，每年耶誕節，他一定會扮耶誕老人來取悅醫院的病童；張醫生年輕時曾愛上一位女友，她因車禍去世，張醫生因而終生未婚。由於他沒有子女，他將遺產送給竹東世光療養院，世光療養院專門照顧智障的孩子，張醫生生前也常抽空去替他們做義工。

　　令大家不解的是張醫生去世的方式，他的車子被人發現停在往五指山的公路旁邊，整個車子朝右，引擎關掉了，鑰匙也被拔出，放在張醫生的右手口袋，座椅傾斜下去，張醫生就如此安詳地在車內去世，醫生認為他死於心臟病突發，可是張醫生卻從來沒有心臟病。在張醫生死亡的前一天晚上，他奇蹟似地救活了一位因車禍而腦充血的小男

◇ pass away (v.) 逝世（名詞形式為 passing）
◇ lament (v.) 哀悼；感嘆
◇ descendant (n.) 後代
◇ bequeath (v.) 遺贈
◇ convalescent (adj.) 康復中的（動詞 convalesce 為「(漸漸)康復」的意思）

Zhang," he said. "This time you're here to stay, right?" I nodded—I wouldn't be leaving Plum Blossom Village again.

Epilogue:

26-28

The Hsinchu-Miaoli edition of the *United Daily News* reports that Doctor Zhang of the Zhudong Veterans' Hospital has passed away. Doctor Zhang worked in the hospital for thirty years. His sudden passing is sorely lamented by all. A lover of children, Doctor Zhang often played games with his patients. Every year at Christmastime, he would dress up as Santa Claus to bring Christmas cheer to the sick boys and girls. In his youth, Doctor Zhang had a girlfriend he loved very much, but she was killed in a car accident; because of this, he never married. Since he has no descendants, he has bequeathed his property to the Light of the World Convalescent Hospital in Zhudong, which is dedicated to caring for mentally handicapped children. Before he died, Doctor Zhang often took time out of his busy schedule to volunteer there.

No one understands exactly how Doctor Zhang died. His car was found parked beside the highway to Five Fingers Mountain, facing right. Doctor Zhang had turned off the engine, removed the key from the ignition and placed it in his right pocket, and leaned his seat back. Just like that, he passed away peacefully in his car. Doctors believe he died of a sudden heart attack, but Doctor

◇ handicapped (adj.)（身體或智力）有障礙的
◇ face (v.) 朝向；面對
◇ engine (n.) 引擎
◇ ignition (n.) 點火開關
◇ lean (v.) 靠

孩，當這個小男孩父親一再感激他的時候，張醫生卻一再地宣稱這不是他的功勞。

　　張醫生的車子向右停，顯示他似乎想向右邊走去，可是公路右邊是一片濃密而深遠的樹林，連一條能步行的小徑都沒有，張醫生究竟想到那裡去呢？這是一個謎。可是從他死去的安詳面容看來，張醫生死亡的時候，似乎有著無限的滿足。

◇ credit (n.)（因功勞而獲得的）讚揚　　　◇ dense (adj.) 稠密的；密集的

Zhang had no history of heart trouble. The night before he died, he miraculously saved a boy from cerebral hyperemia. Though the boy's father thanked him repeatedly, Doctor Zhang insisted that he had no right to take credit.

The fact that Doctor Zhang's car was parked facing right indicates that he meant to head in that direction, but there is nothing on the right side of the highway there but a deep, dense forest without so much as a footpath. Where Doctor Zhang intended to go remains a mystery. Judging by the serene expression on his face, however, he died a perfectly contented man.

◇ mystery (n.) 謎

◇ contented (adj.) 滿意的；知足的

（1）（somewhere or something）is nowhere to be found
找不到（某個東西或地方）（1 段）

But the fountainhead of the immortals is nowhere to be found.

不辨仙源何處尋。

解析

我們慣用 nowhere to be found 來表示「找不到某個東西或某個地方」。它或許一開始就不在那兒，但因為你「找」不到，當然是用 nowhere 加上 to be "found"。

就像我們說到人物一樣。如果有人問你：「這個人是誰？」而你答不出來，就可以說 "No one I know"（我不認識）或 "Nobody important"（無名小卒）。

小試身手

1.　我回到我以為我留下錢包的地方，可是它已不見了。

　　_____

（2）nonetheless 仍然，但是；置於句尾（2 段）

When they brought the boy in, it didn't look too serious, but I had a bad feeling nonetheless.

孩子送來的時候，看上去還不太嚴重，可是當時我就感到有些不妙。

解析

nonetheless 和稍後故事裡出現的 nevertheless 基本上可以互換。這兩個字都是三個單音節字結合而成的複合字（none-the-less），仔細思索這三個字應該可以讓我們猜到複合字的意思——在 nonetheless 所在的字句裡，不會比先前子句所說的現象不真。換句話說，nonetheless 就是強調同等重要的對比。這裡有幾個例子：

◇ 她以為她的面試很糟，但她還是得到了那份工作。
She thought her interview went poorly, but she got the job nonetheless.

◇ 人人都跟他說他不可能成為一個職業籃球選手。然而，他仍然繼續追尋他的夢想。
Everyone told him that he would never become a professional basketball player. Nonetheless, he continued to pursue his dream.

◇ 我累極了，可是我還是撐過了整場會議。
I was extremely tired, but I nonetheless managed to stay awake all through the meeting.

從這三個例子我們更清楚的知道 nonetheless 的意思，也得知 nonetheless 可放在句末、句中和句首。

小試身手

2-1. 我們大概不會贏。雖然如此，我們仍應全力以赴。

_____

2-2. 她脾氣有點暴躁，可是我依然愛她。

_____

---

(3) as 因為(2 段)

When I told the boy's parents that he needed to spend the night in the hospital, they were a bit bewildered, as by all appearances their son looked like he was feeling fine—he even made a little mischief here and there.

我告訴孩子父母，孩子必須住院，他們有點困惑，因為小孩子看上去精神還滿好的，甚至不時做些胡鬧的舉動。

解析

as 雖然是個短短小字，卻代表很多不同的意思。不相信？我來證明給你看：

◇ 我喜歡一邊工作一邊唱歌。——as 表「while」
　I like to sing as I work.

◇ 他絕不會長得跟我一樣高。——as 表示「像」或「如」
　He'll never be as tall as I am.

◇ 她決定最好還是快點離開，因為天色已晚。——as 表示「因為」
　She decided she had better get going as it was getting late.

小試身手

3. 她找不到她以前的方子。

_____

(4) 文法概念：句子開頭的名詞子句（5 段）

The most self-possessed of the family, he comforted his son and his daughter-in-law as best he could.

他是全家最鎮靜的一位，不時安慰兒子和媳婦。

解析

這個句子以名詞子句開端，但這個名詞子句卻非主詞。事實上，這串長句用來形容主詞 he（the grandfather）。英文母語人士在寫作時，為了句型活潑，常常會用這類句型。否則，每個句子都是主詞開頭，豈不單調？你寫作時可以試試看，不一定要用名詞子句，用副詞子句也很好。

4-1. (名詞子句)她紅色的法拉利是整個停車場最漂亮的車,一看就看得到。

_____

4-2. (副詞子句)一大清早我就去公園運動。

_____

(5) virtually 簡直;幾乎 (5 段)

He told me that he and the boy virtually lived for each other.

他告訴我,孩子和他幾乎相依為命。

解析

故事中的男孩真的跟祖父相依為命嗎?換句話説,如果男孩死了,祖父也活不成?相依為命只是一種誇飾法而 virtually 這個字恰好可以強調出那種效果,同時讓你知道那並非「字面上」(literally)的意思。由此可知,virtually 和 literally 是反義的。而 virtually 等同於 practically,有時也可用 all but。

5-1. 過年的時候,台北的路上幾乎沒有什麼人。

_____

5-2. 高三生的生活簡直被準備聯考淹沒了。

_____

(6) judge by... 以……來判定(7 段)

Judging by the look of things, I knew that the boy's chances of survival were very slim.

以目前的情況來看，我相信孩子存活的機會非常小。

解析

這個用法很難說明，可是一看例子就會很清楚。請看以下兩例：

◇ 爺爺看天空的顏色就知道天氣要變壞了。
Grandfather could tell by the color of the sky that bad weather was coming.

◇ 從你的表情看來，我知道你感到心煩意亂。
I can see by the look on your face that you're upset.

例子中的動詞(tell 和 see)跟標題上的 judge 是一樣的功能，都是意指某人如何得出某個結論。by 在本句中是「以」的意思，其所帶領的片語通常接在主要動詞後面、其他部分句子的前面，跟中文語順不一樣。

小試身手

6-1. 聽她的口音就知道她是義大利人。

_____

6-2. 從我空空如也的銀行帳戶看來，我得找一份工作。

_____

(7) take one's leave of ... 和……告別(7 段)

I've lived a full and comfortable life; now I'm ready to take my leave of this world.

我這輩子活得豐富而舒適，我已對人世沒什麼眷戀。

解析

「我活得有意義」的英文說法為：I've lived a meaningful life. ——在 live 後面需加 life 一字，如句中的 live a full and comfortable life。

另外，把 leave 這個動詞當作名詞用，好像有點怪怪的。但這就是慣用語，也不可代換成 leaving。例如：

◇ 當他跟我說我想知道的事情之後，我就跟他告別了。
Once he told me what I wanted to know, I took my leave of him.

這個常見的慣用語只用於書寫，不用於口語。如果你在閱讀時留意一些，這個用法並不難學。

小試身手

7-1. 他和同事們告別後，就獨自去做田野調查。

_____

7-2. 她的人生又長又豐富。

_____

(8) 文法概念：Beginning a sentence with a gerund（動名詞）用
　　 動名詞開啟一個句子（9 段）

After I started my car, I felt a sudden desire to go someplace where
I could get some fresh air. Heeding it, I headed toward Five Fingers
Mountain.

我發動車子以後，忽然想到鄉下去透透氣，於是沿著路向五指山開去。

解析

如果不把上段句子寫成兩句，此句可以表達成...fresh air, so I headed
toward...，但分成兩句讀起來比較具有文學性。heed 是「留意」、「聽從」
的意思。我們都有種種衝動與意欲，我們該聽從那些想法嗎？或我們該依據
理性的思考？不管好壞，「heeding＋受詞」可以看成一個單位，甚至可當
句子的主詞，如同下列各動詞轉化成動名詞一樣：

◇ 她忍不住地啜泣，告訴我們她父親對她的意義有多重大。
　 Weeping uncontrollably, she told us how much her father had meant to
　 her.

◇ 他像瘋子一樣地開車，設法逃離警方。
　 Driving like a maniac, he managed to escape from the police.

◇ 仔細閱讀這本書有助於你的英文能力。
　 Reading this book carefully will help your English.

◇ 他喜歡坐在沙發上邊喝咖啡邊看電視。
　 He loved to sit on the couch drinking coffee and watching TV.

上面第一和第二個句子中的動詞 weep 和 drive 是不及物動詞，所以不須接
受詞。

小試身手

8-1. 找新房子可以很好玩，只要你不用擔心錢的事情。

_____

8-2. 打羽球是很棒的一種運動。

_____

8-3. 揍你的老闆一拳大概不會是個好主意。

_____

8-4. 他們泡在溫泉裡，回憶著小時候一起做過的各種瘋狂事。

_____

(9) 文法概念：despite＋having＋Vpp（10 段）

Despite having driven that road twenty or thirty times before, I'd never noticed any place called Plum Blossom Village.

我這條路已經走過了幾十次，從來不知道有叫李花村的地方。

解析

Despite having studied English for many years, you may have trouble with this structure.——雖然學了多年英文，你可能對此結構還是無法掌握——其實沒那麼難啦，它的意思就是「雖然已經（動詞）過……；雖然（動詞）了（一段時間）……」，要記得 despite 後接 Ving 或名詞，多練習幾次喔。

9-1. 雖然訓練了將近一年，他在跑完馬拉松之前，還是得停下來用走的。

_____

9-2. 雖然已經喝了五杯雞尾酒，他卻沒有醉意。

_____

（**10**）**used to** 的用法（**12** 段）

Rather, it was how the village reminded me of the way the Taiwanese countryside used to look forty years ago.

而是李花村使我想起了四十年前台灣的鄉下。

解析

為何這裡用 used to look，而不用 looked 就好？used to 後接原形動詞，表「過去曾……現在已不再……」，強調出了鄉下看起來已跟以往不同，人們通常在回想從前時，會說 the way it used to be（以前如何如何）。

◇ 他現在或許過胖，可是他以前可是個職業運動員。
He may be overweight now, but he used to be a professional athlete.

◇ 她現在或許虛弱到無法旅行，但她以前每年都會去歐洲度假。
She may be too sick to travel now, but she used to take a vacation to Europe every year.

◇ 我以前會說義大利文，但是我學了中文後就全忘光了。
I used to be able to speak Italian, but I forgot it after I learned Chinese.

10. 台灣以前處於戒嚴的狀態。

_____

（11）not a single + N. 一個（……東西）也沒有（12 段）

There was not a single car—besides walking, the only way to get around was by bicycle.

這裡看不到一輛汽車，除了走路以外，只能騎腳踏車。

解析

single 即表示「單獨一個」，例如：

◇ 如果天空連一朵雲都沒有的話，一定非常晴朗。
   The sky must be pretty clear if there isn't a single cloud in it.

◇ 如果你一整年連一本《壹週刊》都沒看，你一定真的很不喜歡這份雜誌。
   You must really dislike *Next Magazine* if you haven't read a single issue all year.

◇ 如果你一整個月連一片巧克力都沒吃的話，那你的節食一定會成功。
   Your diet must be succeeding if you haven't eaten a single piece of chocolate for a month.

11. 沒有任何好理由開這麼無聊的會。

_____

（12）check on 或 check up on 檢查；確認某人是否無恙（15 段）

I asked the old woman, who was busy in the kitchen, if I could use [her phone] to make a call to Zhudong to check on a patient in the veterans' hospital there.

我問那位在廚房裡忙的老太太，可不可以借用他們的電話打到竹東去，因為我關心竹東榮民醫院的一位病人。

解析

check 是個非常好玩的字。當你住旅館，第一件事就是 check in（辦住房）；如果這是個好旅館，你會四處逛逛設施（check out the amenities）；如果你有孩子，而他們沒跟著一起旅行，你可能會想打電話回家看看他們是否都好（call home and check（up）on them）。最後，你從旅館 check out（辦退房），但是事情還沒完──如果你把疾病帶回家，你還得去找醫生做檢查（go to the doctor for a checkup）。希望這治療不會太貴，要不然，你就得開一張大支票（write a big check）囉！

check 的相關用法	
check（up) on	檢查；確定無恙
check out	看看（俚）
check in/out	辦理住（退）房手續
checkup	（身體）檢查
check	支票（名詞）

小試身手

12. 妳今天不用打電話去關心奶奶，我很確定她沒事。

_____

（13）the way（one came）的用法：來時路（16 段）

I left the village the way I'd come in and drove back to the Zhudong Veterans' Hospital.

沿著進來的路走出李花村，(我)開車回到竹東榮民醫院……

解析

way 有兩個主要含意，可以解釋成「辦法」或「途徑」，本例中就是用「途徑」的意思。「循著原路回去」的英文就說成 the way you came。以下是另外幾個有用的句子，注意修飾 way 的東西常常放在它後面。

◇ 你能告訴我怎麼從台北去基隆嗎？
Can you tell me the way from Taipei to Keelung?

◇ 你走錯路了！
You're going the wrong way!

◇ 從這裡到那裡無法坐車。
There's no way to get from here to there by car.

小試身手

13-1. 你可以給我一些方向嗎？我忘了到你家的路怎麼走。

_____

13-2. 盲人能找到要去的地方，我覺得很了不起。

_____

13-3. 要通到一個男人的心，得先透過他的胃。（要贏得一個男人的心，最好的辦法是給他好吃的東西。）

_____

13-4. 她覺得被困住了，好像沒有出路。

_____

（14）no matter... 無論……（17 段）

I yearned to return to Plum Blossom Village for another visit, but no matter how hard I tried, I couldn't find it again.

我一直想再回李花村看看。可是卻再也找不到李花村了。

解析

matter 在此作動詞用，其實你不用記這個，你只要記住 no matter 就是「無論」或「不管」的意思就行了。no matter 視情況不同後面可能接 who, what, when, where, why 或 how，尤其是 how。例如：

◇ 無論他説什麼，你就是不會相信他。
   No matter what he says, you'll never believe him.

◇ 無論我跑多快，都不及她快。
   No matter how fast I run, I won't be as fast as she is.

注意 "no matter how" ＋adj.＋S.＋V. 這個結構，它的意思是「無論（主詞）（動詞）得多麼（形容詞）」，雖然其義甚明，但是 how 後面緊接形容詞，這個順序還是得留心一下。

小試身手

14-1. 無論我睡幾個小時，隔天總是感到疲倦。

_____

14-2. 不管外面多冷，他仍穿著短褲。

_____

14-3. 無論你去哪裡或做什麼，我永遠會愛你。

_____

（15）on duty 值班（18 段）

Last night, while I was on duty, a boy was brought to the emergency room.

昨天晚上我值班，急診室送來了一個小孩子。

解析

duty 是指「職責」，而值班的時候才有職責，可是 duty 永遠是名詞，不可能是動詞，所以「值班」要怎麼說呢？就用 be＋on duty！等你的職責都做完了，你就可以「下班」，也就是 be＋off duty 表示。

小試身手

15. 警察覺得有責任阻止那個犯人，雖然當時他並沒有值班。

_____

（16）文法概念：without＋sb＋Ving …不用／沒有(某人)……
（18 段）

You can imagine the result without me having to describe it in detail— when the boy was brought in, even his ears were bleeding.

其結果可想而知，他被送進醫院的時候，連耳朵裡都在不斷地流出血來。

解析

英文文法有時很怪對吧？不用我說（without me needing to tell you）大家都知道。without 開頭的片語是副詞子句，形容整個句子。透過以下例子，各位將會更容易明白：

◇ 他沒叫你做的話，你會做嗎？
Would you have done that anyway without him asking you to?

◇ 我們不告訴你怎麼走的話，你能找到那房子嗎？
Can you find the house without us showing you the way?

其實更常見的結構是「without＋Ving」，例如：

◇ 無法上網，她還活得了嗎？
Will she survive without being able to access the Internet?

◇ 希望我這樣說不會很失禮。
I hope I can say this without sounding rude.

我知道你現在在想什麼——「你一定要把『其結果可想而知』搞得這麼複雜嗎？能不能直接把 without 後面那串子直接刪掉？」可以，你是對的。我只是想寫出更優美的句子，同時強調文中男孩的傷勢如此嚴重，糟糕到連醫生都不願描述而已。

小試身手

16-1. 我可以過得好好的，不用你教我怎麼做。

_____

16-2. 要是他唱歌沒走調，合唱團的聲音就會好很多。

_____

16-3. 即使沒有盛裝打扮，她看起來也很美。

_____

16-4. 他們知道如何不花大錢就能玩得好。

_____

(17) straight 直接(18 段)

We took him straight into the operating room…
我們立刻將他送入手術室……

解析

大家應該都知道兩點間的最短距離是一條直線。尤其是在你趕時間的時候，肯定不會拐彎抹角，會直往目的地(go straight where you need to go)。既然這麼急，當然不用三個音節的 directly，而直截了當的用 straight 就好了。所以，我要直接告訴你(I'll just tell you straight up)，straight 可以直接當副詞用，表「直接地」。

小試身手

17-1. 她開門見山切入重點。

_____

17-2. 老師告訴學生，要是他再頂嘴，她就立刻送他去見校長。

_____

17-3. 飛機起飛時必須往前，但是直升機可以直接往上飛。

_____

（18）as long as 只要（19 段）

"As long as this boy lives, I'm willing to die."

「只要小孩子活下去，我可以走。」

解析

「as long as」是夠簡單，也夠有用的一個片語。

◇ 只要盡力過，不管比賽結果如何，你都能怡然自得。
No matter where you finish in a race, you'll be satisfied as long as you gave it your best shot.

◇ 我不管妳嫁給誰，只要他對妳好。
I don't care whom you marry as long as he treats you right.

◇ 只要你表現出你的用心，記得「只要」的英文怎麼說，你大概就不會忘記了。
As long as you put forth the effort to remember how to say "只要" in English, you probably won't forget.

小試身手

18. 只要你能保持幽默感，你就不會一直慘下去。

_____

（19）"with..." 作為副詞子句（25 段）

I parked the car and walked toward the village with a quick step and a light heart.

我將車子停好以後，輕快地走進了李花村。

解析

當你看到 with 的第一個反應，你可能會想它的意思是「和」或「跟」，對不對？但這裡的意思是「有著」、「帶著」的意味，通常可帶領一個副詞子

句。例如：

◇ 我希望死得有尊嚴。
I want to die with dignity.

◇ 她微笑，眼神晶亮地看著我。
She smiled and looked at me with a gleam in her eye.

◇ 吃完極豐盛的晚餐後，我們帶著快樂的心情和飽足的胃回家。
After that magnificent dinner, we all went home with happy hearts and full stomachs.

明白了嗎？這個結構美國人一天到晚在用，如果你也用的很順，一定能給母語人士留下深刻印象。

> **小試身手**
>
> 19-1. 對於生命她懷著全新的感恩之心離開醫院。
>
> _____
>
> 19-2. 我很感興趣地看著那老人做他的奇怪運動。
>
> _____

（20）died of（cause）死於……（27段）

Doctors believe he died of a sudden heart attack.
醫生認為他死於心臟病突發。

解析

人的死亡有各種原因，車禍、肺炎、跳傘意外……都有可能。這時候你可以用「died of＋原因」，可能是某種疾病，像癌症或心臟病等等來說明，亦或是抽象的失戀，如 die of a broken heart 即表示「死於心碎」。

注意不要和 die in 搞混。例如像在 he died in a car crash/he died in the fire/he died in his car 這些句子中，我們可以得知 in 是用於描寫死亡時的場景，而非原因。

小試身手

20-1. 她爺爺抽了一輩子的香菸，最後死於肺癌。

_____

20-2. 他出了車禍，死於嚴重頭部外傷。

_____

20-3. 他死於那場車禍。

_____

（21）without so much as a/an... 連一個……也沒有（28 段）

But there is nothing on the right side of the highway there but a deep, dense forest without so much as a footpath.

可是公路右邊是一片濃密而深遠的樹林，連一條能步行的小徑都沒有。

解析

聰明的讀者應該會發現這個結構很像解析11的「not a single N」結構。如果你禿頭禿到一根頭髮都沒了，那你就可以用 without so much as a strand of hair 來形容。當然，如果有人連一個友善的問候都沒有（without so much a friendly hello），就直接說某人禿頭，會讓人覺得很沒禮貌！

注意這裡可以用 without a single... 來代替 without so much as...，如果想要語氣更強的話，就可以寫成 without so much as a single...。

小試身手

21-1. 那房間空無一物，連一張草蓆也沒有。

_____

21-2. 學生根本沒有基本的地理知識就畢業。

_____

小試身手解答

1. I went back to where I thought I had left my purse, but it was nowhere to be found.

2-1. We probably won't win. Nonetheless, we should still do our best. 或 We probably won't win, but we should do our best nonetheless.

2-2. She has a bit of a short temper, but I love her nonetheless.

3. She could not find her old house as the whole neighborhood had changed since she moved away.

4-1. The best-looking car in the parking lot, her red Ferrari was easy to spot.

4-2. Early in the morning, I got up and went to the park to exercise.

5-1. During Lunar New Year, there is virtually/practically no one on the streets of Taipei.(本句不能代入 all but)

5-2. High school seniors' lives are all but consumed by preparations for college entrance exams.(本句可用 literally 或 practically 代換 all but)

6-1. You can tell by her accent that she's Italian.

6-2. Judging by the emptiness of my bank account, I need to get a job.

7-1. He took his leave of his colleagues and set out to do field research alone.

7-2.　She lived a long and productive life.

8-1.　Looking for a new house can be fun as long as you don't have to worry about money.

8-2.　Playing badminton is a great form of exercise.

8-3.　Punching your boss is probably not a good idea.

8-4.　They soaked in the hot springs, reminiscing about all the crazy things they did together when they were kids.

9-1.　Despite having been trained for almost a year, he still had to stop and walk before finishing the marathon.

9-2.　Despite having had five cocktails, he didn't feel drunk.

10.　Taiwan used to be under martial law.

11.　There is not a single good reason to have (或 hold) such a boring meeting.

12.　You don't need to call and check on Grandma today—I'm sure she's fine.

13-1. Can you give me some directions? I've forgotten the way to your house.

13-2. I think it's amazing that blind people can find their way around.

13-3. The way to a man's heart is through his stomach.

13-4. She felt trapped—there seemed to be no way out.

14-1. No matter how many hours I sleep, I always feel tired the next day.

14-2. No matter how cold it is outside, he still wears shorts.

14-3. No matter where you go or what you do, I will always love you.

15.　The police officer felt that it was his responsibility to stop the criminal, even though he was off duty at the time.

16-1. I can get by just fine without you telling me what to do.

16-2. The choir would sound a lot better without him singing off key.

16-3. She looks beautiful even without dressing up.

16-4. They know how to have a good time without spending a lot of money.

17-1. She got straight to the point.

17-2. The teacher told her student that if he talked back again, she would send him straight to the principal's office.

17-3. A plane has to go forward when it takes off, but a helicopter can go straight up.

18.　As long as you can keep a sense of humor, you'll never stay miserable for long.

19-1. She left the hospital with a new appreciation for life.

19-2. I watched with interest as the old man did his strange exercises.

20-1. Her grandfather smoked cigarettes his whole life and eventually died of lung cancer.

20-2. He had a car accident and died of severe head trauma.

20-3. He died in the car accident.

21-1. The room was bare without so much as a mat.

21-2. Students are graduating without so much as a basic knowledge of geography.

The Boy from a Distant Land
來自遠方的孩子

1-5　作為大學的歷史系教授，即使不兼任何行政職務，仍要參加各種校內外會議。今年我總算有一個休假一年的機會，我選了普林斯頓大學作為我休假的地方。

剛來的時候，正是暑假，雖然有些暑修的學生，校園裡仍顯得很冷清，對我而言這真是天堂，我可以常常在校園裡散步，享受校園寧靜之美。

就在此時，我看到了那個孩子，他皮膚黑黑的，大約十三、四歲，一看上去就知道是中南美洲來的，他穿了 T 恤，常常在校園裡閒逛。令我有點不解的是，他老是一個人，在美國，雖然流行個人主義，但並不提倡孤獨主義，青少年老是呼朋引伴而行，像他這樣永遠一個人閒逛，我從來沒有見過。

我不僅在校園裡看到他，也在圖書館、學生餐廳，甚至書店裡看到他。我好奇地注意到，他不僅永遠一個人，而且永遠是個旁觀者，對他來講，似乎我們要吃飯，要上圖書館等等都是值得他觀察的事。可是他只觀察，從不參與。比方說，我從未看到他排隊買飯吃。

CD1-4
◇ administrative duties 行政職務；行政工作
◇ sabbatical (n.) 休假(大學教授每隔幾年可休一年的假)
◇ Princeton University 普林斯頓大學
◇ deserted (adj.) 空無一人的
◇ stroll (v.) 漫步；閒適地走
◇ tranquil (adj.) 恬淡安靜的
◇ dark-skinned (adj.) 皮膚黝黑的
◇ saunter (v.) 閒步；閒逛
◇ individualism (n.) 個人主義
◇ fashionable (adj.) 時髦的；流行的
◇ loner (n.) 獨行俠
◇ spot (v.) 察覺；發現

Being a history professor, even without taking on any administrative duties, I have to go to all sorts of meetings both on and off campus. But this year I finally had the chance to take a sabbatical. I chose to spend it at Princeton University.

It was summer vacation when I arrived, and although there were a few summer students, the campus seemed pretty deserted. To me, it was pure heaven. I'd often stroll around the campus, enjoying its tranquil beauty.

That was the first time I saw the boy. Dark-skinned, probably thirteen or fourteen years old, he was obviously from Central or South America. He wore a T-shirt and was always sauntering leisurely around the campus. I didn't really understand why he was always alone—in America, individualism may be fashionable, but being a loner isn't. Young people tend to travel in groups—he was the first person I'd ever seen who always walked alone.

It wasn't just on the campus grounds that I'd see him—I spotted him in the library, the student cafeteria, even the bookstore. Curiously, I noticed that not only was he a loner, but a perpetual onlooker as well: it seemed that in his eyes, the way we ate or went to the library were subjects worthy of his observation. But he would only watch—he never took part. For example, never once did I see him standing in line to buy food.

◇ perpetual (adj.) 永久的；不停歇的
◇ onlooker (n.) 旁觀者
◇ subject (n.) (尤指可供研究或觀察的) 主體或題材
◇ worthy (adj.) 值得的 (其後常接介詞 of)
◇ observation (n.) 觀察

有一次，我到紐約去，在帝國大廈的頂樓，我忽然又看到了他，這次他對我笑了笑，露出一嘴潔白的牙齒。當天晚上，在地鐵車廂裡，我又看到了他，坐在我的後面，車廂裡只有我們兩個人。

6-10 我開始覺得有些不可思議，他為什麼老是尾隨著我？

秋天來了，普林斯頓校園內的樹葉，一夜之間變成了金黃色的，我更喜歡在校園內散步了，因為新英格蘭秋景，美得令人陶醉，可是令我不解的是，這位男孩子仍在校園內閒逛，唯一的改變是他穿了一件夾克。所有的中學都已經開學了，難道他不用上學嗎？如果不上學，為什麼不去打工呢？

有一天，我正要進圖書館去，又見到了他，他斜靠在圖書館前的一根柱子上，好像在等我，我不禁自言自語地問：「搞什麼鬼，他究竟是誰？怎麼老是在這裡？」

沒有想到他回答了，「教授，你要知道我是誰嗎？跟我到圖書館裡去，我會告訴你我是誰。」令我大吃一驚的是他竟然用中文回答

◇ the Empire State Building 帝國大廈(位於美國紐約市，在世界貿易中心雙塔遭恐怖份子攻擊倒塌後，成為紐約市最高建築物)
◇ reveal (v.)露出；顯露
◇ subway (n.)地鐵

One time, when I went to New York, I saw him on top of the Empire State Building. This time he smiled at me, revealing a mouth full of pearly white teeth. On the subway that evening, I saw him again, sitting behind me; we were the only two people in our section of the train.

"This is getting unbelievable," I thought. Why was he always following me?

6-10

Autumn came, and the leaves on the Princeton campus turned gold overnight. I enjoyed my walks through the campus even more, for autumn in New England is intoxicatingly beautiful. But I didn't understand why the boy still wandered around the campus exactly as he had before (only now with a jacket). Classes had started at all the middle schools—why didn't he have to go to school? If he wasn't in school, why didn't he get a job?

One day, as I was about to go into the library, I saw him yet again. He was leaning against a pillar in front of the library as though he were waiting for me. I couldn't help mumbling to myself, "What is with this kid? Who is he, and why is he always here?"

Much to my surprise, he answered me, "Professor, do you want to know who I am? Follow me into the library and I'll tell you." I was

---

◇ section (n.) 區段；部分
◇ overnight (adv.) 一夕之間 (注意：此字
　是副詞，別誤以為是名詞)
◇ intoxicatingly (adv.) 令人陶醉地

◇ pillar (n.) (大型建築物的) 柱子
◇ mumble (v.) 喃喃而語；含糊不清地說
　話

我。他一面回答我，一面大模大樣地領我向查詢資料的一架電腦走去。

我照著他的指示，啟用了一個多媒體的電腦系統，幾次以後，這個男孩子告訴我，我已找到了資料；這是一卷錄影帶，一按鈕以後，我在終端機看到了這卷錄影帶，這卷錄影帶我看過的，去年我服務的大學舉辦「飢餓三十」的活動，主辦單位向世界展望會借了這卷錄影帶來放，這裡面記錄的全是世界各地貧窮青少年的悲慘情形，大多數的鏡頭攝自非洲和中南美洲，事後我又在電視上看到一次，今天我是第三次看了。

11-15　雖然這卷錄影帶上的場景都很令人難過，可是我印象最深的是一個少年乞丐的鏡頭，他坐在一座橋上，不時地向路邊的人叩頭。說實話，雖然我看了兩次這卷錄影帶，別的鏡頭我都不記得了，可是這個男孩不停地叩頭的鏡頭，我卻一直記得。

大概五分鐘以後，那個少年乞丐叩頭的鏡頭出現了，我旁邊的這個孩子叫我將錄影帶暫停，畫面上只有那個小乞丐側影的靜止鏡頭，然

◇ stunned (adj.) 錯愕的；詫異的
◇ stride (v.) 大步走
◇ confidently (adv.) 有自信地
◇ instruction (n.) 指示
◇ multimedia (adj.) 多媒體的

◇ locate (v.) 找到……的位置
◇ 30-Hour Famine 飢餓三十（一個人道關懷的社會運動，參加者連續 30 小時不進食，以體驗餓肚子的感受）
◇ sponsor (n.) 主辦者

stunned to hear him answer me in Chinese. As he spoke, he strode confidently over to a library search computer with me in tow.

Following his instructions, I started up a multimedia computer system; after a few searches, the boy told me I'd located the information he was looking for. It was a video that began playing on my computer terminal at the push of a button. I'd seen it before—last year, the university where I taught held a "30-Hour Famine", and the main sponsor of the event, World Vision Taiwan, had played the video for everyone there. It was full of images of poverty-stricken young people all over the world, especially in Africa and Latin America, where most of the scenes were filmed. Later on, I saw it again on TV; this was the third time I'd seen it.

Although all the scenes in the video were heartbreaking, the one that had made the deepest impression on me was a shot of a young beggar sitting on a bridge, periodically kowtowing to the people who passed by. In fact, despite having seen the video twice before, I'd forgotten all the other scenes, but the image of the kowtowing boy had stayed with me.

11-15

About five minutes later, the scene appeared. The boy beside me told me to pause the video there, at a frame where all you could see

◇ image (n.) 影像；畫面
◇ film (v.) 拍攝（成影片）
◇ scene (n.) 景象；（電影或戲劇裡的）幕
◇ heartbreaking (adj.) 令人心碎的
◇ shot (n.) 鏡頭；景

◇ periodically (adv.) 不定期地；偶爾
◇ kowtow (v.) 磕頭
◇ frame (n.) （影片、底片、光碟等記錄影像的）一格；（亦可指每一個定格所呈現的）畫面

後他叫我將畫面選擇性地放大，使小乞丐的側影顯得非常清楚。

他說，「這就是我」。

我抬起頭來，看到的是一個健康而且笑嘻嘻的孩子，我不相信一個小乞丐能夠有如此大的變化。

我說：「你怎麼完全變了一個人？」

16-20　孩子向我解釋：「自從世界展望會在巴西拍了這段記錄片以後，全世界都知道巴西有成千上萬的青少年流落街頭，巴西政府大為光火，所以他們就在大城市裡大肆取締這些青少年乞丐。這些警察非常痛恨我們，除了常常將我們毒打一頓以外，還會將我們帶到荒野裡去放逐，使我們回不了城市，很多小孩子不是餓死，就是凍死在荒野裡。

「有一天，我忽然發現大批警察從橋的兩頭走過來，我看到了一個孩子被他們拖到橋中間痛揍，我當時只有一條路走，那就是從橋上跳下去。」

◇ enlarge (v.) 放大
◇ profile (n.) 身影；身形
◇ dramatically (adv.) 戲劇化地；急遽地
◇ documentary (n.) 紀錄片
◇ upset (adj.) 不安的；不高興的
◇ underage (adj.) 不足齡的；未成年的

was a side view of the motionless beggar boy. Then he told me to select and enlarge that part of the screen so that the beggar's profile was crystal clear.

"That's me," he said.

I lifted my head to look at him, but what I saw was a healthy, happy boy. I couldn't believe a beggar could have changed so dramatically.

"How is it that you look like a totally different person now?" I asked.

The boy answered, "As soon as World Vision filmed this documentary in Brazil, the whole world knew that there were thousands of youth living in the streets there. The Brazilian government was very upset at this, so they cracked down hard on underage beggars in the cities. The police absolutely despised us— they didn't just beat us. Sometimes they even took us out to the middle of nowhere and abandoned us, so we couldn't get back to the city. A lot of kids either starved or died of exposure out there."

16-20

"One day, I suddenly became aware that two big groups of policemen were coming toward me from opposite sides of a bridge. I saw them drag a kid to the middle of the bridge and start beating him up. There was only one way to escape: by jumping off the bridge."

◇ despise (v.) 鄙夷；藐視
◇ exposure (n.) 暴露於（風霜雨雪）
◇ opposite (adj.) 相反的
◇ escape (v.) 逃離；脫逃

我嚇了一跳，「難道你已離開了這世界？」

他點點頭，「對，現在是我的靈魂和你的靈魂談話，至於這個身體，僅僅是個影像，並不是什麼實體，我活著的時候，一直羨慕別人有這種健康的身體，所以我就選了這樣的身體，你摸不到我的，別人也看不到我，也聽不到我們的聲音，因為靈魂的交談是沒有聲音的，你難道沒有注意到你我的嘴唇都沒有動，我其實不會中文，可是你卻以為我會中文。」

我終於懂了，怪不得他從來不吃飯，現在回想起來，我甚至沒有看到他開過門。

21-25　雖然我在和一個靈魂談話，我卻一點也不害怕，他看上去非常友善，不像要來傷害我。

「你為什麼選上我？」

「你先結束這個電腦系統，我們到外面去聊。」

我們離開了校園，走到了一個山谷，山谷裡有一個池塘，山谷裡和池塘裡全是從北方飛過來的野鴨子，我們找了一塊草地坐下。

「我離開這個世界以後，終於到了沒有痛苦，也沒有悲傷的地

◇ illusion (n.) 幻影；錯覺
◇ exist (v.) 存在
◇ migrate (v.) (尤其指鳥類或獸類的) 遷徙
◇ patch (n.) 一片／塊 (地)

I started with shock. "You don't mean to say that you've already left this world?"

He nodded. "Yes—right now my spirit is speaking to your spirit. This body is a mere illusion; it doesn't really exist. When I was alive, I always envied people who had healthy bodies like this—that's why I chose this body. You can't touch me, and no one else can see me or hear my voice because conversation between spirits makes no sound. Haven't you noticed that our lips have never moved? I can't really speak Chinese, but to you it sounds like I can."

I finally understood. No wonder he never ate—now that I thought about it, I had never even seen him open a door before.

Although I was talking to a spirit, I felt no fear at all. He looked quite friendly—it didn't seem like he had come to hurt me.

21-25

"Why did you choose me?"

"First, shut down the computer system. Let's talk outside."

We left the campus and walked to a valley where there was a pond. Both valley and pond were full of wild ducks that had migrated there from the north. We found a patch of grass and sat down.

"After I left this world, I finally found a place free from suffering and sorrow. But in spite of that, I still ran into countless poor people.

◇ suffering (n.)痛苦；折磨　　　　　◇ sorrow (n.)悲痛；悲哀

方。雖然如此，我仍碰到不知道多少個窮人，大家聊天以後，公推我來找你。你是歷史學家，你有沒有注意到，我們人類的歷史老是記錄帝王將相的故事，從來不會記錄我們這些窮人的故事，也難怪你們，畢竟寫歷史的人都不是窮人，你們根本不知道我們的存在，當然也無法從我們的眼光來看世界了。

26-30　「世界上所有的歷史博物館，也都只展覽皇帝、公爵、大主教這些人的事跡，我在全世界找，只找到一兩幅畫，描寫我們窮人。拿破崙根本是個戰爭販子，他使幾百萬人成為無家可歸的孤兒寡婦，可是博物館裡老是展覽他的文物。

　「你們中國歷史有名的貞觀之治，在此之前，短短幾十年內，你們的人口因為戰亂，只剩下了百分之十。百分之九十的人都是餓死的，可是你們歷史教科書也只輕描淡寫地一筆帶過這件大事。

　「我最近也開始看《世界地理雜誌》，這份雜誌所描寫的地球，是個無比美麗的地方，他們介紹印度的時候，永遠介紹那些大理石宮

- ◇ historian (n.)歷史學家
- ◇ emperor (n.)皇帝
- ◇ general (n.)將軍；將領
- ◇ noble (n.)貴族
- ◇ exhibit (v.)展示；展出
- ◇ artifact (n.)文物；藝品
- ◇ duke (n.)公爵
- ◇ archbishop (n.)大主教；樞機主教
- ◇ warmonger (n.)戰爭販子
- ◇ widow (n.)寡婦

We talked with one another for a while, and they decided to send me here to see you. You're a historian—have you ever noticed how human history is filled with accounts of emperors, kings, generals and nobles, but it never records what happens to us poor people? We can't blame you—after all, history has never been written by the poor. You're not even aware that we exist, so it's only natural that you don't know how to see the world through our eyes."

"History museums the world over exhibit nothing but artifacts   26-30
from people like emperors, dukes and archbishops. I've looked all over the world, but I've only found a couple paintings of us poor people. Napoleon was nothing but a warmonger—he made millions of people homeless widows and orphans, but museums are always displaying his papers and personal effects."

"In Chinese history, you have your famous Prosperity of Zhenguan. But during the few decades before that, the ravages of war reduced your population to a tenth of what it had been before. Ninety percent of the people starved to death, but your history textbooks just gloss over the whole thing."

"Lately I've been reading *World Geography Magazine*. The world it describes is such a beautiful place! When they report on India, they

◇ display (v.) 展示；展覽
◇ personal effects 個人物品；私人用品
◇ Prosperity of Zhenguan 貞觀之治（唐朝盛世）
◇ decade (n.) 十年

◇ ravage (s) (n.) 破毀；殘敗 (the ravages of war 即戰亂、烽火的殘跡、損害)
◇ reduce (v.) 降低；減少
◇ gloss (over) (v.) 掩蓋；掩飾

殿，而從來不敢拍一張印度城市裡的垃圾堆，以及在垃圾堆旁邊討生活的窮人，他們介紹里約熱內盧，也只介紹海灘上游泳的人，而不敢介紹成千上萬露宿街頭的兒童。」

「你也許覺得我們的校園好美，我們現在坐的地方更加美，可是世界真的如此之美嗎？你只要開車一小時，就可以到達紐澤西州的特蘭登城，這個城裡黑人小孩子十二歲就會死於由於販毒而引起的仇殺，如果他不是窮人，他肯在十二歲就去販毒嗎？」

「我們死去的窮人有一種共識，只要歷史不記載我們窮人的事，只要歷史學家不從窮人的眼光來寫歷史，人類的貧窮永遠不會消失的。」

31-35　　「我們希望你改變歷史的寫法，使歷史能忠實地記載人類的貧困，連這些來自北方的野鴨子，都有人關心，為什麼窮人反而沒有人關心呢？」

我明白了，可是我仍好奇。

「這世界上的歷史學家多得不得了，為什麼你們會選上了我？」

◇ showcase (v.) 陳列；展示
◇ marble (n.) 大理石
◇ palace (n.) 宮殿；皇宮
◇ trash heap 垃圾堆
◇ drug-dealing (n.) 毒品交易；販毒
◇ vendetta (n.) 世仇

showcase the marble palaces, but they never have the courage to take a picture of a trash heap in an Indian city or the poor people trying to eke out a living beside it. When they talk about Rio de Janeiro, they mention the people swimming at the beaches, but they never have the guts to talk about the homeless children in the streets."

"Maybe you think our campus is lovely, and the place where we're sitting now is lovelier still. But is the world really this beautiful? All you have to do is drive for an hour and you'll be in Trenton, New Jersey, a city where twelve-year-old black children are killed in drug-dealing vendettas. Would a twelve-year-old sell drugs if he wasn't poor?"

"We deceased poor people have come to the conclusion that as long as history doesn't record anything about us—as long as historians don't write history through our eyes—human poverty will never go away."

"We hope you'll change the way history is written so that it faithfully records human poverty. Even these ducks from the north have people who care about them—why does no one care about the poor?"

31-35

I understood, but there was one more thing I wanted to know.

"There are so many historians in the world—why did you choose me?"

◇ deceased (adj.) 死亡的　　　　　　◇ faithfully (adv.) 忠實地；詳實地
◇ conclusion (n.) 結論

「因為我們窮人對你有信心，知道你不會因為同情窮人而挑起再一次的階級鬥爭，我們只希望世人有更多的愛，更多的關懷，我們不要再看到任何的階級仇恨。」

我點點頭，答應了他的請求。他用手勢謝謝我。然後他叫我往學校的方向走去，不要回頭，一旦我聽到他的歌聲，他就會消失了。

36-39　一會兒，我聽到了一陣笛聲，然後我聽到了一個男孩子蒼涼的歌聲。從前，我在念大學的時候，參加了山地服務團，正好有緣參加了一位原住民的葬禮。葬禮中，我聽到了類似的蒼涼歌聲。

幾分鐘以後，我聽到了一個女孩子也加入了歌聲，終於好多人都參加了，大合唱的歌聲四面八方地傳到我的腦中，我雖然聽不懂歌詞，可是我知道唱的人都是窮人，他們要設法告訴我，這個世界並不是像我們看到的如此之美。我現在在秋陽似酒的寧靜校園裡散步，我的世界既幸福又美好，可是就在此時，世界上有很多窮人生活得非常悲慘，只是我不願看到他們而已。我知道，從此以後，在我的有生之年，每當夜深人靜的時候，我就會聽到這種歌聲。

◇ empathy (n.)移情作用；感同身受
◇ provoke (v.)挑起；激起
◇ warfare (n.)戰爭；戰事
◇ antagonism (n.)對立；對抗
◇ gesture (v.)比手勢；用肢體動作表示
◇ flute (n.)笛子

"Because we have faith in you: we know that you won't use your empathy for the poor to provoke more class warfare. We only want people to love more, to care more; we don't want to see any more class antagonism."

I nodded, promising to do what he had asked. He gestured to thank me. Then he told me to walk back toward the school without turning around. The moment I heard him start singing, he would be gone.

Soon after, I heard the sound of a flute, and then the desolate voice of a boy. Back when I was in college, I did some service among Taiwanese aborigines, and one time I had an opportunity to attend one of their funerals. The singing I heard there was similar.   36-39

A few minutes later, I heard a girl's voice join in. Eventually many voices joined in, and their chorus poured into my mind from all directions. Although I didn't understand the words, I knew that all the singers had been poor. They were trying to tell me that the world was not as beautiful as what I saw. As I walked through the campus under the wine-colored autumn sun, my world was happy and beautiful. But even at that moment, there were multitudes of poor people living in misery—it was just that I had been unwilling to see them. I knew then that on every quiet night for as long as I lived, I would hear music like theirs.

◇ desolate (adj.) 淒涼的；冷清的　　◇ chorus (n.) 合唱
◇ aborigine (s) (n.) 原住民　　◇ multitude (n.) 群眾
◇ funeral (n.) 葬禮　　◇ misery (n.) 不幸；苦難

　　公元二千一百年，世界歷史學會在巴西里約熱內盧開會，這次大會有一個特別的主題，與會的學者們要向一位逝世一百年的歷史學家致敬，由於這位來自台灣學者的大力鼓吹，人類歷史不再只記錄帝王將相的變遷，而能忠實地反應全人類的生活，因此歷史開始記錄人類的貧困問題，歷史文物博物館也開始展覽人類中不幸同胞的悲慘情形。

　　這位教授使得人類的良心受到很大的衝擊，很多人不再對窮人漠不關心，也由於這種良知上的覺醒，各國政府都用盡了方法消除窮困。這位歷史學家不僅改變了寫歷史的方法，也改寫了人類的歷史。

◈ conference (n.)(代表)大會
◈ attendance (n.)出席；參加
◈ respects (n.)問候；致意
◈ vicissitude (s)(n.)興衰浮沉

◈ historical artifact (s)(n.)歷史文物
◈ wretchedness (n.)不幸
◈ prick (v.)刺痛
◈ indifferent (adj.)冷漠；冷淡

It is the year 2100, and the World Historical Society is holding a conference in Rio de Janeiro, Brazil. The conference has a special theme: the scholars in attendance are paying their respects to a historian who died a hundred years earlier. Because of this Taiwanese scholar's tireless efforts, human history no longer merely recorded the vicissitudes of emperors, kings, generals and nobles, but began to faithfully reflect the lives of all humankind. Because of him, history started taking note of the problem of human poverty, and museums of historical artifacts started using their exhibits to show the wretchedness of the less fortunate.

This professor truly pricked the conscience of humanity. Multitudes of people ceased being indifferent to the plight of the poor, and due to this massive moral awakening, governments in all nations began making genuine efforts to eliminate poverty. This historian didn't just change the way history was written—he rewrote human history.

◇ plight (n.) 苦境
◇ moral awakening 道德（良知）覺醒
◇ genuine (adj.) 真正的
◇ eliminate (v.) 消滅；掃除
◇ rewrite (v.) 改寫

(1) off and on campus 校內外 (1 段)

Being a history professor, even without taking on any administrative duties, I have to go to all sorts of meetings both on and off campus.

作為大學的歷史系教授，即使不兼任何行政職務，仍要參加各種校內外會議。

解析

以上的英譯有幾個重要的東西，最主要的是「校內校外」，用 on and off campus 表示。其他的有 take on (any) administrative duties「擔任行政職務」和 go to all sorts of meetings「參加種種的會議」。

> **小試身手**
>
> 1. 下學期有一連串熱鬧歡樂的校內活動。
>
> _____

(2) take a sabbatical 休假 (1 段)

But this year I finally had the chance to take a sabbatical. I chose to spend it at Princeton University.

今年我總算有一個休假一年的機會，我選了普林斯頓大學作為我休假的地方。

解析

上帝連續用六天時間創造世界之後，覺得第七天應該是休息的時候了，所以他在這天停工休息。這時把什麼事情都擱下，利用這天檢討過去一個禮拜的缺失或休息以待下星期繼續打拼，從宗教的角度看，稱之為 Sabbath「安息日」。讀者在本重點所見到的 sabbatical 即由 Sabbath 演變而來，但在此處特別指大學教授在從事研究教學若干年後所享有的一年期休假，稱之為 sabbatical year。

2.　在某些大學院校，教授們每隔七年有一年休假。

_____

(3)　(be) pure heaven 極好；真是天堂；只應天上有（2 段）

To me, it was pure heaven.
對我而言這真是天堂。

解析

天堂應該是很美好的地方吧？否則為什麼任何宗教都勸人為善，好讓人在過完凡塵今生後，直登天堂或西方極樂世界呢？所以，若有機會到一個讓你感到萬分舒適的情境或者秀麗優美的地方，不妨大聲說：Oh, this is pure heaven!。

3.　在夏威夷小島度假兩週，真是愜意之至。

_____

(4)　subjects worthy of observation 值得觀察的題材（4 段）

Curiously, I noticed that not only was he a loner, but a perpetual onlooker as well: it seemed that in his eyes, the way we ate or went to the library were subjects worthy of his observation.
我好奇地注意到，他不僅永遠一個人，而且永遠是個旁觀者，對他來講，似乎我們要吃飯，要上圖書館等等都是值得他觀察的事。

解析

worthy of 是重要的片語，作「值得」、「具……價值」解釋。因此 worthy of observation 就是「值得觀察」、「具觀察價值」的意義。而 subjects worthy of observation 即指「值得觀察的主體」、「具觀察價值的對象」之意。

小試身手

4. 她認為凡事皆關乎政治，不管是國內國外、或小或大的，都是值得她觀察的主題。

_____

(5) intoxicatingly beautiful 美得令人陶醉(7 段)

I enjoyed my walks through the campus even more, for autumn in New England is intoxicatingly beautiful.

我更喜歡在校園內散步了，因為新英格蘭秋景，美得令人陶醉。

解析

文學上常使用到修辭誇飾的技巧，例如美則美矣，中文有時誇張到「美得冒泡」的地步。至於把美的境界提升到「陶醉」、「醉人」則是東西方都有的手法。原文說「美得令人陶醉」，譯文對之以 intoxicatingly beautiful，用副詞 intoxicatingly 來提升形容詞 beautiful，美到令人沉醉，想當然是美到極點了。

小試身手

5. 我找不到適當的字眼來形容那種令人屏息的美景。

_____

(6) with someone in tow 某人尾隨在後（9 段）

As he spoke, he strode confidently over to a library search computer with me in tow.

他一面回答我，一面大模大樣地領我向查詢資料的一架電腦走去。

解析

tow 無論作動詞或名詞解，都是「拖曳」、「拖拉」的意思，因此片語 in tow 當然就有「跟在後面」、「尾隨其後」之意，而自然也就是「有某人跟在後面」的意思。

小試身手

6. 小丑走在前面唱著歌，而一群小孩蹦蹦跳跳尾隨其後。

_____

(7) at the push of a button 按按鈕（10 段）

It was a video that began playing on my computer terminal at the push of a button.

這是一卷錄影帶，一按鈕以後，我在終端機看到了這卷錄影帶。

解析

名詞 button 指的是任何鈕扣或按鈕狀的東西，鈕扣當然是 button，可是任何儀表機器上的按鈕也是用 button 表示。順帶補充，肚臍正名叫作 navel，俗名卻是 belly button，好玩吧！

小試身手

7. 有這麼威力強大的毀滅性武器，世界可能在一按鈕間就沒了。

_____

（8）make the deepest impression on someone 令某人印象至 為深刻（11 段）

Although all the scenes in the video were heartbreaking, the one that had made the deepest impression on me was a shot of a young beggar sitting on a bridge, periodically kowtowing to the people who passed by.

雖然這卷錄影帶上的場景都很令人難過，可是我印象最深的是一個少年乞丐的鏡頭，他坐在一座橋上，不時地向路邊的人叩頭。

解析

這個重要而實用的片語應該很容易學起來，可以先拆裝再重新組合：給某人（on someone）製造或留下（make/leave）深刻的印象（a deep impression），最後的結果當然就是 make/leave a deep impression on someone。

小試身手

8. 她卓越的分析能力給我留下了深刻的印象（我對她卓越的分析能力印象深刻）。

　　＿＿＿＿＿＿＿＿＿＿＿＿＿＿＿＿＿＿＿＿＿＿＿＿＿

（9）　crack down（hard）on 掃蕩；嚴厲取締（16 段）

The Brazilian government was very upset at this, so they cracked down hard on underage beggars in the cities.

巴西政府大為光火，所以他們就在大城市裡大肆取締這些青少年乞丐。

解析

動詞 crack 是指像鞭子之類的東西，所發出如「劈」或「啪」的清脆響聲。crack a whip 是指以前馬車駕駛在空中揮舞鞭子，即使沒有打到馬匹，也可讓馬兒加速前行。crack 也可表示「裂開」的意思，如核桃或雞蛋之類的外殼裂開。這些地方的 crack 都表示施加力量（壓力）於某物。所以，當公權力

對於不法情事，以雷霆般的聲勢展開強力作為時，就使用 crack 這個字，再搭配 down on，甚至再添上副詞 hard，就更加傳神了，但是不甚好學，請讀者要費一些苦心。

9. 新任警察局長誓言要加強取締在這一地帶發生的任何不法情事。

_____

(10) take someone out to the middle of nowhere 把某人帶到一個不知名的地方（16 段）

The police absolutely despised us—they didn't just beat us. Sometimes they even took us out to the middle of nowhere and abandoned us, so we couldn't get back to the city.

這些警察非常痛恨我們，除了常常將我們毒打一頓以外，還會將我們帶到荒野裡去放逐，使我們回不了城市。

解析

片語 the middle of nowhere 指的是「前不著村，後不著店」的地方，也就是所謂的「荒郊野外」。因此，take someone out to the middle of nowhere 就表示「把某人帶到荒郊野外」。這種用法不算難，讀者只要把 the middle of nowhere 揣摩透徹，就可運用自如。

10. 爺爺的家在荒郊野外，每次我們開車到那邊都要好幾個小時。

_____

（11） die of exposure 因受風吹日曬雨淋而亡（16 段）

A lot of kids either starved or died of exposure out there.

很多小孩子不是餓死，就是凍死在荒野裡。

解析

食、衣、住是人能夠生存的三大基本需求。以英文表示，food 為「食」，clothing 為「衣」，那「住」呢？一般用 shelter 表示，指的是能夠讓人不受風吹日曬雨淋的「棲身之處」。一個人若失去了棲身之處，就沒有「住」的屏障了，名詞 exposure 就在表達這種情況。所以，片語 die of exposure 即在表示「暴露於風霜雨雪而亡」。

小試身手

11. 因為沒有棲身之處而死的人比餓死的人還多。

_____

（12） beat someone up 把某人痛扁一頓（17 段）

I saw them drag a kid to the middle of the bridge and start beating him up.

我看到了一個孩子被他們拖到橋中間痛揍。

解析

動詞 beat 指「毆打」，介系詞 up 則有「完」、「盡」的意味，因而整個片語 beat someone up 強烈予人一種「打到爽」、「揍個夠」、「痛扁一頓」的感覺。

小試身手

12. 我被拉到角落去，然後遭到一頓毒打。

_____

(13) start with shock 嚇一跳（18 段）

I started with shock. "You don't mean to say that you've already left this world?"

我嚇了一跳，「難道你已離開了這世界？」

解析

在這裡再次向讀者強調，許多英文單字常是一字多義的現象。所以，當閱讀到 start 這個字時，不要先入為主就認定它是「開始」的意思。現在給這個字多添加一些色彩，start 這個字也指當人在碰到一些突如其來的情況、措手不及、心頭或整個人「猛然一震」的狀態。如今在 start 之後加上 with shock，更是直指「嚇一大跳」。

小試身手

13. 當一個影子閃過窗戶時她嚇了一跳。

_____

(14) feel no fear at all 一點都不感到害怕（21 段）

Although I was talking to a spirit, I felt no fear at all.

雖然我在和一個靈魂談話，我卻一點也不害怕。

解析

feel 是個很有趣的字，它可以當連綴動詞，後面接形容詞；也可以是及物動詞，後面跟著名詞，作受詞用。

舉例來說，想要表達「我感到害怕。」可以說 I feel afraid. 或 I feel fear.此處英譯以 I feel no fear at all. 來詮釋「(我)一點都不感到害怕。」除了用 no 還加上 at all 來發揮出「一點都不」的意味。如果讀者想用形容詞來表達「害怕」，那同樣的句子可改寫為：I don't feel afraid at all.

小試身手

14. 這種事我經歷多次了，所以一點都不感到害怕。

　　　　　　　　　　　　　　　　　　　　　　　　　　　　　　　　

---

(15) 語法觀念：關係副詞和關係代名詞所構成的形容詞子句
...where ... ；...that ...(24 段)

We left the campus and walked to a valley where there was a pond. Both valley and pond were full of wild ducks that had migrated there from the north.

我們離開了校園，走到了一個山谷，山谷中有一個池塘，山谷中和池塘裡全是從北方飛過來的野鴨子。

解析

在以上的英譯中，我們可以發現到兩種構造不同、但一樣都是形容詞性質的子句。where there was a pond 是由關係副詞 where 所引導的形容詞子句，作用在修飾子句之前的名詞 a valley；that had migrated there from the north 則是由關係代名詞 that 所引導的形容詞子句，修飾子句之前的名詞 wild ducks。既然兩者都是形容詞子句，好奇心重的讀者也許會有此一問：where 的位置是否可以用 that 取代，而 that 的位置是否也可以用 where 取

代？答案都是不可以替換。這牽涉到 where 和 that 的性質各自不同。雖然兩者都是從屬連接詞，但 where 具副詞性質，以原句而言，它就在修飾 there was a pohd，表「地點」；that 具代名詞性質，一般作為子句的主詞或受詞，以原句而言，它就扮演著 had migrated 這個動作的主詞。以上的概述雖然簡要，卻是相當重要的文法觀念，讀者宜多思考。

小試身手

15-1. 我找到一家圖書館，在那裡睡了一整個下午的覺。

_____

15-2. 這就是咬過郵差的那條狗。

_____

（16）free from... 沒有……；免於……（25 段）

After I left this world, I finally found a place free from suffering and sorrow.

我離開這個世界以後，終於到了沒有痛苦，也沒有悲傷的地方。

解析

這個片語基本上作「免於……」解釋。人類四大自由中，有「免於匱乏的自由」和「免於恐懼的自由」，英文原文分別為 freedom from want 和 freedom from fear。心思縝密的讀者應該可以發現，中譯「的自由」其實是贅詞，這兩個英文所表達的其實就是「免於匱乏」和「免於恐懼」，僅此而已。

小試身手

16. 烏托邦是個沒有煩憂、沒有痛苦的地方。

_____

(17) the world over 全世界；世界各地(26 段)

History museums the world over exhibit nothing but artifacts from people like emperors, dukes and archbishops.

世界上所有的歷史博物館，也都只展覽皇帝、公爵、大主教這些人的事跡。

解析

讀者們在國中時代即學過 all over the world「世界各地」，應該人人都琅琅上口，因為唸起來很順。其實英文另有幾個片語可以表達類似的意思，如 across the world、throughout the world、in every part of the world、everywhere in the world 或此句的 the world over 都是。

小試身手

17. 全球各地的人們都要面對地球暖化的威脅。

_____

(18) nothing but... 只(不過是)……(26 段)

Napoleon was nothing but a warmonger—he made millions of people homeless widows and orphans, but museums are always displaying his papers and personal effects.

拿破崙根本是個戰爭販子，他使幾百萬人成為無家可歸的孤兒寡婦，可是博物館裡老是展覽他的文物。

解析

nothing but... 是很有意思的一個片語。nothing 為「什麼都不是」之意，關鍵在 but 這個介詞，它當「除了……」。因此 nothing 和 but 兩字的結合，結果就是「除了……之外，什麼都不是」的意思，亦即中文常說的「只(不過是)……」或「根本就是……」。

小試身手

18. 他只不過是個吹牛大王。

_____

---

(19) a tenth of... 十分之一的 (27 段)

But during the few decades before that, the ravages of war reduced your population to a tenth of what it had been before.

在此之前，短短幾十年內，你們的人口因為戰亂，只剩下百分之十。

解析

數學的分數，英文該怎麼表達呢？英譯用 a tenth (of) 來表示「十分之一」(即原文裡的「百分之十」)。「十分之二」則是 two tenths。很合理吧，因為「十分之二」是「兩個十分之一」。那十分之三呢？當然就是「三個十分之一」，所以就是 three tenths 囉！

最後把分數的英語表達法整理如下：

(一)先分子後分母(註：和中文表達法正好相反。)

(二)分子使用基數詞(註：即 one, two, three, four 之類的字。)

(三)分母使用序數詞(註：即 third, fifth, sixth, seventh, eighth 之類的字。)

(四)分子大於一時，分母要用複數。例如「三分之一」為 a third，而「三分

之二」為 two thirds。

(五)習慣上「二分之一」用 a half 表示,「四分之一」以 a quarter 表示。

小試身手

19. 四分之三的蛋糕被吃掉了。

_____

---

(20) gloss over the whole thing 粉飾太平;力圖遮掩(27 段)

Ninety percent of the people starved to death, but your history textbooks just gloss over the whole thing.

百分之九十的人都是餓死的,可是你們歷史教科書也只輕描淡寫地一筆帶過這件大事。

解析

gloss 作名詞時指光滑物體表面所呈現的「光彩」或「光芒」。在本解析重點的片語 gloss over the whole thing 裡,gloss 是動詞,表示動手腳把有瑕疵的物體表面加以處理,讓它像完美的東西一樣光彩奪目,可惜雖然金玉其外,仍然是敗絮其中。因此 gloss over the whole thing 這個片語即指把整個事件加以美化,企圖掩人耳目,就如中文的成語「粉飾太平」。

小試身手

20. 無論我怎麼極力掩飾那件事情,他仍然存疑。

_____

（21） eke out a living 勉強維生（28 段）

When they report on India, they showcase the marble palaces, but they never have the courage to take a picture of a trash heap in an Indian city or the poor people trying to eke out a living beside it.

他們介紹印度的時候，永遠介紹那些大理石宮殿，而從來不敢拍一張印度城市裡的垃圾堆，以及在垃圾堆旁邊討生活的窮人。

解析

make a living 和 earn a living 是讀者們都相當熟悉的片語，那麼 eke out a living 呢？應該比較傷腦筋吧。其實它和前兩個片語相去不遠，如果說有什麼明顯差異的話，那就是 eke out 比較有「勉強掙得」的意味，所以 eke out a living 指的是「很辛苦才能維持溫飽」的意思。

小試身手

21. 像這樣一個不景氣的時代，我認為我能勉強溫飽已算幸運了。

_____

（22） have the guts to V 有勇氣……；有膽子……（28 段）

When they talk about Rio de Janeiro, they mention the people swimming at the beaches, but they never have the guts to talk about the homeless children in the streets.

他們介紹里約熱內盧，也只介紹海灘上游泳的人，而不敢介紹成千上萬露宿街頭的兒童。

解析

想要學會這個實用而且非常口語的英文，得先把重點放在 guts 這個字。它本來指的是人體裡的五臟六腑，在這裡則指的是「勇氣」、「膽識」。因此，片語 have the guts to V 指的是「有勇氣膽識去做某事」。只是，有時候光

憑血氣之勇仍不足以成大事，除了具備勇氣膽識(have the guts)，還要足智多謀(have the brains)，智勇兼備，才更有成功的希望。

小試身手

22. 智勇兼備的人更有可能成功。

_____

(23) **come to the conclusion that...** 所得到結論為……；所下的定論是……(30 段)

We deceased poor people have come to the conclusion that as long as history doesn't record anything about us—as long as historians don't write history through our eyes—human poverty will never go away.

我們死去的窮人有一種共識，只要歷史不記載我們窮人的事，只要歷史學家不從窮人的眼光來寫歷史，人類的貧窮永遠不會消失的。

解析

名詞 conclusion 作「結論」、「定論」，因而片語 come to the conclusion that... 意為「得到……的共識」或「有……的定論」。要特別注意，從 that 之後是個子句，表示這個共識或結論的事實。至於動詞部分，除了用 come to 也可以選擇使用片語 arrive at 或動詞 reach 來表達相同的意思。

小試身手

23. 我們的定論是有錢不是萬能，沒有錢萬萬不能。

_____

(24) the way S + V ... ……的方法(31 段)

We hope you'll change the way history is written so that it faithfully records human poverty.
我們希望你改變歷史的寫法，使歷史能忠實地記載人類的貧困。

解析

讀者可以從英譯得知，這個 the way history is written 可以拆解成 the way 和 history is written 兩部分。前者 the way 是名詞，作動詞 will change 的受詞，後者 history is written 則是個子句，前面省略了介詞 in 和關係代名詞 which。the way 作先行詞時，後面的關係代名詞 which 很少表現出來。譯文用 the way history is written 來傳達「歷史的寫法」，以下還有幾個「……的手法／樣子」的例子，請參考練習。

小試身手

24-1. 人們喜歡她的一切：她說話的樣子，她唱歌的樣子，她跳舞的樣子，她的一顰一笑。

_____

24-2. 即使現代科學家也對建造金字塔的方法讚嘆不已。

_____

(25) multitudes of... 成千上萬的……；為數眾多的……(37 段)

As I walked through the campus under the wine-colored autumn sun, my world was happy and beautiful. But even at that moment, there were multitudes of poor people living in misery—it was just that I had been unwilling to see them.
我現在在秋陽似酒的寧靜校園裡散步，我的世界既幸福又美好，可是就

在此時，世界上有很多窮人生活得非常悲慘，只是我不願看到他們而已。

解析

國中時代學過好幾百(hundreds of...)，好幾千(thousands of...)之類的片語，如果要表示「成千上萬」，則説 hundreds of thousands of... 或 tens of thousands of...。本解析重點裡的片語 multitudes of... 也差不多是相同的意思。其實，multitude 這個名詞本身即可指數以千百計的人群，數量龐大可觀。因此，multitudes of people 當然就是指很多很多人囉！

小試身手

25. 成千上萬的人們，老的少的、男的女的、貧的富的，都擠在廣場想要一睹奇觀。

_____

(26) pay one's respects to... 向某人致意；對某人致敬(38 段)

The conference has a special theme: the scholars in attendance are paying their respects to a historian who died a hundred years earlier.
這次大會有一個特別的主題，與會的學者們要向一位逝世一百年的歷史學家致敬。

解析

讀者可有注意到「尊敬」(respect)還特別使用複數形(respects)，由此可見，除了原有的「尊敬」，也跟著多出了「追思悼念」的意味。注意，只有對已去世的人，才用 pay respects，對於活著的人表示尊敬要用 show respect。另外，我們向某人道賀，用的也是複數形式的 Congratulations! 向某人致上最深沉的哀悼之意，就用 my deepest condolences。

26. 她在她老師的葬禮短暫停留致意。

_____

(27) be indifferent to... 對(人)冷淡；對(事)漠不關心(39 段)

Multitudes of people ceased being indifferent to the plight of the poor, and due to this massive moral awakening, governments in all nations began making genuine efforts to eliminate poverty.

很多人不再對窮人漠不關心，也由於這種良知上的覺醒，各國政府都用盡了方法消除窮困。

解析

既然多數讀者在國中就學過 be interested in...「關心……」，在高中學過 be enthusiastic about...「熱衷……」，這個片語 be indifferent to... 即指「對……冷漠」。請看以下兩例：

◇ 他們更注重(關心)建立一個完備的制度。
　 They are more interested in the establishment of a sound system.

◇ 他熱衷各種運動。
　 He is enthusiastic about all kinds of sports.

小試身手

27. 在我們之中有太多人對世界的問題冷漠，因為它們對我們並沒有直接影響。

_____

小試身手解答

1. There will be a series of exciting activities on campus next semester.

2. At certain colleges, professors are given a sabbatical every seven years.

3. The two-week-long holiday at a small Hawaiian island was pure heaven for me.

4. She considers anything related to politics, whether domestic or foreign, minor or major, a subject worthy of observation.

5. I can't find words to describe the breathtaking beauty of the scenery.

6. The clown walked in front singing a song, with a crowd of hopping and skipping kids in tow.

7. With weapons of such enormous destructive power, the world could end at the push of a button.

8. Her excellent analytical ability left a deep impression on me.

9. The newly appointed police chief swore to crack down on any illegal activities taking place in this neighborhood.

10. Grandpa's house is in the middle of nowhere—it takes us several hours to drive there.

11. More people died of exposure than of starvation.

12. I was pulled into a corner and beaten up.

13. She started with shock when a shadow flitted past the window.

14. I felt no fear at all because I had been through this sort of thing many times.

15-1. I found a library, where I spent the whole afternoon taking a nap.

15-2. This is the dog that bit the mailman.

16. A utopia is a place (which is) free from worry and pain.

17. People the world over will have to face the threat of global warming.

18. He is nothing but a braggart.

19. Three quarters of the cake was eaten.

20. No matter how hard I tried to gloss over the matter, he remained skeptical.

21. In a recession like this, I consider myself fortunate to be able to eke out a living.

22. Those with brains as well as guts are more likely to succeed.

23. We have arrived at the conclusion that not everything is possible with money, but nothing is possible without it.

24-1. People like everything about her—the way she talks, the way she sings, the way she dances, the way she smiles and the way she frowns.

24-2. Even modern scientists marvel at the way the pyramids were built.

25. Multitudes of people, young and old, male and female, rich and poor, crowded together in the square to see the spectacle.

26. She stopped by her teacher's funeral to pay her respects.

27. Too many of us are indifferent to the world's problems because they don't impact us directly.

Train Surfing

飆　車

1-5　　再過一分鐘，我就要跳下去了。

　　我生長在巴西的一個農村，從小就幫我的爸爸種田，念過一年的書，就不念了。可以說我幾乎只認識幾個字，好在鄉下孩子人人都是如此。

　　村子裡有一條鐵路經過，每天都有火車走過，我好羨慕坐火車的人，也有時會幻想火車去的地方。說起來慚愧，從前我只知道鄉下地方長什麼樣子，其他地方我就完全不知道了。

　　十七歲那年，我開始也在村子裡找些零工，是替人蓋房子的粗活。我這才知道，做工是可以賺錢的，每次賺了錢，我都給了我媽媽。

　　有一天，我在田裡做工的時候，村長帶了一個人來，這位先生穿著體面，他向我走近，摸摸我的手臂，甚至叫我張開口，讓他看看我的牙齒。我感到有點被侮辱，可是不敢在村長面前表現出來，因為村長是大家尊敬的人，他識字——有一部腳踏車，也常替我們村裡解決問題。

CD1-6

◇ （標題）surf (v.) 衝浪；此指「為了追求刺激與快感，在某個快速移動的物體（如火車）上面保持平衡的動作」

◇ Brazilian (adj.) 巴西的

◇ luckily (adv.) 幸虧

◇ rural (adj.) 鄉下的

◇ railroad (n.) 鐵路，railroad track 為鐵軌

◇ track (n.) 軌道

One minute from now, I'll jump.

1-5

CD1-5

I was born and raised in a Brazilian farming village. I started helping my dad in the fields when I was just a child. I only went to a year of school before I quit; it's fair to say that I can only read a few words. Luckily, every other child who grew up in a rural area is the same way.

There was a railroad track that passed through our village, and every day there were trains that ran along it. I envied the people on the trains so much! Sometimes I'd try to imagine where the trains were going. It's a little embarrassing to admit, but it used to be that all I knew was the countryside—I didn't know a thing about anyplace else.

The year I turned 17, I got my first part-time job, doing rough work as a house builder in the village. That was how I learned that I could make money by working. Each time I got paid, I'd give the money to my mom.

One day as I was working in the fields, the village leader showed up with a well-dressed man I didn't know. The man walked up to me, felt my arms with his hands and even asked me to open my mouth so he could have a look at my teeth. I felt a little humiliated, but I didn't dare show it in front of the village leader—everyone respected him because he could read, he owned a bicycle and he often solved problems for the village.

◇ envy (v.) 羨慕；嫉妒
◇ countryside (n.) 鄉下
◇ rough (adj.) 粗活的，需要體力的
◇ well-dressed (adj.) 穿著體面的

6-10　　當天晚上，爸爸告訴我，城裡有一家營造商來鄉下找工人，他們看中了我，怪不得那位先生要親自檢查我的體格夠不夠強壯，我本來就很強壯，最近一年，常要搬運磚頭和水泥，又壯了很多。我當然立刻答應去城裡工作，誰也不願意一輩子在鄉下種田的。

　　村裡的神父知道我要遠行，趕來看我。他說了一大堆話，年輕人最不喜歡別人囉嗦，我已記不得他講什麼了，可是回想起來，他曾說了一句話，他勸我不要羨慕別人，我當時不懂這是什麼意思。

　　我很快就懂了神父的意思，我在鄉下種田的時候，從不羨慕別人，因為大家都是一樣的，我們的玩伴們都不識字，也無此需要。到了城裡，當我站在鷹架上做工的時候，大多數的街上行人都穿著西裝，拿著手提箱，他們都是在「辦公室」裡工作的，不像我們，必須在烈日下工作。

　　我知道他們念過書，會認字，我沒有念過書，也不識字，這就是不同的地方。

◇ humiliate (v.) 使⋯⋯丟臉
◇ construction company (n.) 建設公司
◇ tough (adj.) 結實的；耐勞的；強壯的
◇ brick (n.) 磚

◇ ages (n.) 很長的時間(口語)
◇ long-winded (adj.) 囉嗦的
◇ urge (v.) 力勸
◇ jealous (adj.) 嫉妒的

That night, my dad told me that a construction company from the city had come to our village to look for workers. They had their eye on me—that was why the man had come to make sure I was built tough enough. I had always been strong, and all the bricks and cement I had moved this past year had made me even stronger. Of course, I jumped at the chance to work in the city—no one wants to spend his whole life planting fields on a farm.

When he learned that I was going away, the village priest came to see me. He talked for ages! Teenagers hate it when people are long-winded—I've already forgotten everything he said. Now that I think of it, though, I do remember him urging me not to envy others. At the time, I had no idea what he meant.

But it wasn't long before I understood. Back in the village, I had never been jealous of anyone because everyone was the same—none of my playmates could read, and none of them needed to. But in the city, while I was working up on the scaffolding, most of the people passing through the street below were wearing suits and carrying briefcases. They all worked in "offices," not under the scorching sun like us.

I knew they had gone to school and could read. But I hadn't been to school, and I couldn't read. That was the difference.

◇ playmate (n.) 玩伴
◇ scaffolding (n.) 鷹架
◇ briefcase (n.) (硬殼的)公事包，手提箱

我開始羨慕別人了。我羨慕所有念過書，會認字的人。

11-15　　我們工寮裡有一架機器，領班每天都在機器前敲敲打打，也會利用機器印出一些東西。他們告訴我，這就是電腦。我很想玩這部電腦，可是我沒有念過書，不可能用電腦的。

　　我的領班告訴我，我領的薪水不能再放在工寮裡，他帶我去一家銀行。我搞了半天，才弄懂什麼叫銀行。領班帶我去開戶，那位行員抬起頭來，對我看了一眼，立刻說：「你可以到第三十二號窗口去辦。」原來三十二號窗口是專門替不識字的人設立的，有行員替我們這種人填單子。幸好領班事先替我填好了單子，不需要去第三十二號窗口，可是為什麼行員立刻就知道我不識字呢？我為了到銀行去，還刻意穿了最好的衣服。

　　大約三個月前，我們工地裡來了一些警察，和領班談了一陣子，走了，什麼事也沒發生。

　　原來當地發生了兇殺案，被殺的人顯然和人吵架，對方竟然將他打

◇ scorching (adj.) 灼熱的
◇ barracks (n.)（士兵或工人住的）棚屋；工寮
◇ foreman (n.) 工頭；領班
◇ button (n.) 鈕；鍵
◇ stash (v.) 藏；存放（口語）
◇ wage (n.) 薪資
◇ figure out (v.) 弄清楚；理解
◇ counter (n.) 櫃檯
◇ apparently (adv.) 顯然地

I started to feel jealous of others. I was jealous of everyone who had gone to school and could read.

There was a machine in our barracks that the foreman would sit in front of every day, hitting buttons and printing things out. I was told it was a computer. I really wanted to play around with the computer, but my lack of schooling made that impossible.

Our foreman told me that I couldn't keep stashing all my wages in our barracks, and he took me to a bank. It took me quite a while to figure out what exactly a bank was. When the foreman brought me there to open an account, the bank teller lifted up her head, gave me a look and said, "You can go to counter 32 to open your account." Apparently counter 32 was set up for people who couldn't read— there was an employee there who would fill out forms for them. Fortunately, the foreman had already filled out the form for me, so I didn't have to go to counter 32. But how had the bank employee been able to tell so easily that I couldn't read? I had made sure to wear my best clothes to the bank.

About three months ago, some police officers came to our work site, had a talk with the foreman, and then left without incident

It turned out that there had been a murder in the area. The victim

---

◇ set up (v.) 設立
◇ employee (n.) 員工
◇ fill out (v.) 填寫(表格等)
◇ fortunately (adv.) 幸好

◇ site (n.) 地點
◇ incident (n.) 事件；事變
◇ murder (n.) 謀殺案
◇ victim (n.) 受害者

死了，警察到我們工地裡來問有沒有工人晚上出去，領班告訴他工人第二天一早要工作，早就睡覺了。警察才離去，我問領班為什麼警察無緣無故地懷疑我們，他說殺人的傢伙一定是個壯漢，否則不會空手將對方打死的，而我們這些工人卻個個都是壯漢，難怪警察會想到我們。

　　我常常想，如果我識字多好，識了字，我就變成了另一種人，一種大家比較看得起的人。有一天，我做了一個夢，夢到我在教兒子認字。夢醒以後，我幾乎再也睡不著了，因為我知道我已十八歲，再也不能回去念書了。

　　我被警察懷疑的那件事，令我當天氣憤不已，因為我從小就是個乖孩子，從不和人打架，爸爸不准我這麼做，這也是我被村長介紹到城裡來工作的原因。沒有想到，只因自己是個粗壯的工人，就被警察懷疑。

16-20

　　有一次，我的一位好友忽然為了一些小事和街上的一名路人打了起來，還好被我們拉開，否則對方真可能被他打傷。我的這位好朋友

◈ quarrel (n.) 爭執；吵架
◈ antagonist (n.) 敵手；對頭
◈ suspect (v.) 懷疑(某人犯了罪)；起疑
◈ apparent (adj.) 明顯的
◈ murderer (n.) 兇手
◈ bare (adj.) 空的；裸的

had gotten into a quarrel, and his antagonist had beaten him to death. The police had come to ask if any of our workers had been out that night. The foreman told them that we'd all fallen asleep long before the crime since we had to work the next day. Then the police left. I asked the foreman why they suspected us for no apparent reason, and he said that the murderer must have been big and tough; otherwise, he wouldn't have been able to beat the victim to death with his bare hands. All of us workers were big, tough guys, so it was natural that the police would suspect us.

I often thought how great it would be if I could read. If I could read, I'd become a different kind of person, one that people would respect more. One night I dreamed that I was teaching my son to read. When I woke up, I almost couldn't fall asleep again—I was already 18, and I knew that I'd never have another chance to go back to school.

Being suspected by the police that day really made me angry. I'd always been a good boy, and I'd never picked a fight with anyone— my dad wouldn't let me. That was why the village leader had set me up with a job in the city. I never thought that I'd be suspected of a crime just because I was a big, tough worker.

16-20

One day, one of my good friends got in a fight with a guy on the street over some little disagreement. He was lucky that we held him back—otherwise he might have hurt the guy. This friend of mine had

◇ pick a fight (v.) 挑釁打架；故意和人過不去
◇ disagreement (n.) 意見不合

脾氣一直很好，為什麼會忽然發作呢？我懂的，他和我一樣，一直感到人家瞧不起他，打架卻是得到別人尊重的一個辦法。事後，我問我的好友，過去他打過架沒有？他說他是鄉下來的，從來不曾打過架，這一次，他卻有一個衝動，他要打贏來過癮一下，就算可能會被警察抓，他當時已經管不了了。

當天，輪到我做彎鋼筋的工作，這種工作很少人喜歡的，因為彎鋼筋要費很大的力氣。說也奇怪，我將我的一股怨氣，完全發洩在鋼筋上，幾十條鋼筋，我一個人兩小時就全部弄彎了。

不久，我參加了火車的飆車族。這是個新玩意兒，玩的人全是窮年輕人。我們站在火車頂上，努力平衡自己，當然一不平衡，命就沒了。我們這些年輕的建築工人常要走鷹架，因此特別會平衡自己，我們這個工地，人人都去飆過，沒有一個人出過事。

一開始的時候，我們都從慢車開始飆，這叫做初級飆車。警察不准我們在火車靠站時就爬到火車頂上去，所以我們就買一張火車票，完

◇ good-tempered（adj.）脾氣好的
◇ constantly（adv.）不斷地
◇ look down on（v.）看不起
◇ impulse（n.）衝動

◇ pleasure（n.）樂趣
◇ disregard（v.）不理會；不放在心上
◇ risk（n.）風險
◇ rod（n.）棒；條

always been good-tempered—why did he suddenly lose his temper? Then I realized: just like me, he constantly felt how others looked down on him, but if he fought, he'd get respect. Afterward, I asked my friend if he'd ever fought with someone before. He said he was a country boy who had never been in a fight, but this time he felt a sudden impulse to enjoy the pleasure of beating someone. Caught up in the moment, he completely disregarded the risk that he'd be caught by the police.

That day it was my turn to bend steel rods, which is a job almost nobody likes because it's so physically exhausting. Strange to say, I took out all my anger on the steel—working alone, I bent dozens of rods in just two hours.

Not long after that, I started hanging out with the train surfers. Train surfing is a new thing—the people who do it are all poor teenagers. We stand on top of a train and do our best to keep our balance—of course, if anyone ever loses his balance, he loses his life too. Since we young construction workers have to walk on scaffolding, we can balance ourselves with the best of them. Everybody at our work site has train surfed before, and no one's had an accident yet.

We surfed the slow trains at first—that's what we call "beginning surfing." The police won't let us climb on top of the trains when

◇ exhausting (adj.) 令人筋疲力盡的
◇ hang out (v.) 閒晃
◇ balance (n., v.) 平衡

◇ accident (n.) 意外
◇ beginning (adj.) 初級的

全合法的上了車，火車開動了以後，我們紛紛從窗口爬上火車頂。在火車頂上站著真是爽得厲害，年輕人都喜歡速度感，我們窮人沒有汽車，也買不起機車，站在火車頂上，恐怕最能滿足我們的速度感了。

21-25　　對我而言，飆車的原因是可以肯定自己的價值，我一直覺得有些自卑感，因為我不識字，而且一輩子也不會被人尊重，可是飆車的時候，我感到我好厲害。我相信我的飆車夥伴一定也是和我一樣，要藉由飆車讓人家瞧得起我們。

　　飆完慢車以後，有人就會進步到飆快車，站在快車上，感覺更加好了。起初我們很多同伴都不敢飆快車，可是我們究竟還是學會了。有一次，站在我前面的一位飆車手一不小心掉了下去，我也因此休息了一陣子，不久，我又去飆車了。

　　有一次，我遇見一位非常勇敢的飆車手，站在火車要經過的陸橋上，火車通過路橋的時候，他會往下跳，這當然是危險到了極點的動作，可是他成功了，沒有丟掉性命。

　　我決定也要這樣跳一次，我不敢告訴任何人，因為我的朋友們一定

◇ board (v.) 登(飛機、火車等)
◇ legally (adv.) 合法地
◇ exhilarating (adj.) 令人快活的
◇ thrill (n.) 刺激；快感

◇ affirm (v.) 證明
◇ inferior (adj.) 次等的；較差的
◇ awesome (adj.) 了不起；讚(口語)
◇ guts (n.) 膽子；魄力

they're close to a station, so we buy a train ticket, board the train legally and then climb out the windows and onto the top once the train gets going. Standing on top of the train is exhilarating—teenagers love the thrill of going fast. We're too poor to buy cars or motorcycles, so surfing trains is the best way we've got to satisfy our need for speed.

21-25

My personal reason for train surfing is to affirm that I have value. Not being able to read makes me feel sort of inferior. I know that others will never respect me, but when I'm surfing a train, I feel like I'm awesome. I suppose my fellow train surfers are the same: they do it to gain others' respect.

After surfing the slow trains for a while, some of us moved up to the fast ones. Standing on a fast train feels even cooler. A lot of our buddies didn't have the guts to surf the fast trains, but we learned to do it anyway. One time, a guy surfing in front of me lost his concentration and fell off. That convinced me to take a break for a while, but soon I was train surfing again.

Then one day, I met the gutsiest train surfer of all. He'd stand on a bridge over the track, waiting for a train to come. When one came, he'd jump down on it. Of course, it was extremely dangerous, but he managed to do it without getting himself killed.

I decided that I wanted to pull off a jump like that—just once. I

◇ concentration (n.) 專心
◇ convince (v.) 說服
◇ gutsy (adj.) 大膽的

◇ pull off (v.) 成功做到（驚險或困難的動作）

會勸我不要冒這種危險。我悄悄地找到了一部慢車，每個週日早上五點發車，五點五十分會經過一座陸橋，陸橋高度不高，就在我們工寮附近，我甚至還站在橋墩上演練過往下跳的準備動作。

昨天晚上，我忽然想起去教堂祈禱，教堂裡只有一些老太太在念玫瑰經。我這個年輕人進來祈禱，引起一位白髮蒼蒼的老神父的注意，他過來問我：「孩子，你有什麼問題嗎？」我一慌之下，隨口說：「神父，我要遠行了，請神父祝福我。」好心的神父把手放在我的頭上，畫了十字，我放心了。

26-30　　今天是週日，我起了一個大早，來到這座陸橋，橋上靜悄悄地，只有我一個人。我不在乎有沒有人看到我，我只要自己能肯定自己。

現在，我站在橋上，太陽正好升起，火車已在遠處出現，再過一分鐘，我就要往下跳了。

後記：

巴西有一陣子風行火車飆車，很多年輕人因此喪生，也曾經引起國際媒體的注意，飆車族清一色地來自貧民窟，很顯然的，他們在尋求

◇ rosary (n.) 玫瑰經　　　　　　　◇ blessing (n.) 祝福
◇ blurt out (v.)(沒有思考就)衝口說出　◇ validate (v.) 證明(這裡指自己的價值)

didn't tell anyone because I knew my friends would urge me not to take such a huge risk. Quietly, I found a slow train that left the station Sunday mornings at 5 and passed under a bridge at 5:50. The bridge wasn't too high, and it was close to our work barracks. I even practiced standing on the edge of the bridge and getting ready to jump.

Last night, it suddenly occurred to me that I should go to a chapel to pray. Except for a few old ladies praying the rosary, no one was there. Being a young man, I caught the eye of a white-haired old priest when I went in to pray. He came over and asked me, "Is something troubling you, child?" Caught off guard, I blurted out, "Father, I'm going on a long journey. Will you give me a blessing?" The kind priest put his hands on my head and made the sign of the cross. My nervousness disappeared.

26-30

It's Sunday today. I got up early in the morning and came to this bridge. It's very quiet—I'm the only one here. I don't care if anyone sees me—I just want to validate myself.

Now, as the sun rises, I'm standing on the bridge. The train has just appeared in the distance. One minute from now, I'll jump.

Postscript:
For a time, train surfing was quite popular in Brazil, and a lot of young people lost their lives as a result. Eventually the phenomenon

◇ eventually (adv.) 慢慢地；終於　　　◇ phenomenon (n.) 現象

自我肯定和尊敬。

我國的火車，已經電氣化了。兩根連接桿，將火車及高壓線連了起來，因此各位讀者可以放心，不會有年輕人看了我的文章以後去飆火車的。

我們誰都不願看到年輕人去飆任何的車，可是也不妨設法去了解為何這些年輕人要飆車。

◇ slum (n.) 貧民窟　　　　　　　◇ high-voltage (adj.) 高電壓的
◇ yearn for (v.) 非常渴望　　　　◇ vehicle (n.) 車；交通工具

attracted the attention of the international media. Every last one of the train surfers came from the slums; it was obvious that they were yearning for validation and respect.

The trains in our country are now electrified: two linking cables connect the train to high-voltage power lines above. Therefore, there is no need to worry that any young people here will try train surfing after reading my story.

None of us want to see young people surfing trains or any other kind of vehicle, but it certainly wouldn't hurt for us to stop and think about what motivates them to do it.

◇ motivate (v.) 給……動機(去做某事)

(1)（be）born and raised 生長（2 段）

I was born and raised in a Brazilian farming village.
我生長在巴西的一個農村。

解析

要用一個英文字來表示「生長」是不可能的，因為「生長」包括兩個部分：
出生（to be born）和成長（to grow up），尤其 to be born 一定是被動語態，所
以會被拿來與同樣為被動語態的 to be raised（被養育成人）相提並論，而非
主動語態的 to grow up。此外不論正式或非正式的英文中，都常看到（be）
born and raised 這個實用片語，舉例如下：

A: Where're you from?
B: Mississippi, born and raised. (口語用法)
A: 你打哪兒來的？
B: 密西西比州，我在那兒出生長大。

此片語在故事中屬較為正式的用法。

小試身手

1. 我生長在台灣的中央山脈。

_____

(2) pass through 經過
    run（指車輛）走（3 段）

There was a railroad track that passed through our village, and every day
there were trains that ran along it.
村子裡有一條鐵路經過，每天都有火車走過。

解析

英文母語人士不會說一條鐵路或高速公路「位於」某一城鎮，因為鐵路和高速公路都很長，不會只存在於單一城鎮裡，而會說某鐵路或公路「通過」許多鄉鎮、城市，甚至是不同州。動詞片語 pass through 也可用來表示人或車輛沿著街道或公路移動，例如：

A: Will you be staying in Cincinnati tonight?
B: Nope, we're just passing through.
A：你們今晚會住在辛辛那提嗎？
B：不會喔，我們只會開車經過那裡。

此外，run 在英文中的意思與用法多如繁星，在文中是指「(交通工具)行駛」之意，口語中也常可說成「走」，但要小心不要與 walk 混淆，例如：

◇ 763 公車行經此路。
　The 763 bus runs along this road.

◇ 今天是慢遊日；有行駛的火車不多。
　Today is a slow travel day; there aren't many trains running.

另有一延伸用法，當你轉動汽車鑰匙，引擎應該就會 run（運轉、發動）。如果車子拋錨，就可以說 It won't run.（發不動）。事實上，許多機器設備，如洗碗機、馬桶、工廠的生產機具、洗衣機等，都可與動詞 run 連用。大家一定要時時注意常見字詞的「新」用法，就會發現其實可以用簡單的字來表示很多意思喔。

順帶補充一點，修飾道路、鐵軌時，run through 常可與 pass through 替換使用。

小試身手

2-1. 如果我們要待在這裡一段時間，你引擎為什麼沒熄火？

_____

2-2. 七號公路穿過許多高山峻嶺。

_____

2-3. 她是個流浪者，一直是過客，永不停駐。

_____

（3）用連字號創造的複合形容詞（5 段）

One day as I was working in the fields, the village leader showed up with a well-dressed man I didn't know.

有一天，我在田裡工作的時候，村長帶了一個人來，這位先生穿著體面。

解析

英文有個好玩的地方，只要以「 - 」(連字號)連接不同單字後，可以創造出新的形容詞。在故事裡出現過的例子有：

part-time	部分時間的，兼差的
well-dressed	穿著體面的
long-winded	囉嗦的
good-tempered	脾氣好的
high-voltage	高電壓的

上述複合形容詞除了 long-winded 比較難猜以外，其他複合形容詞的意思，只要你了解兩個單字的意思，就可輕易從字面上猜出其義。熟能生巧，所以多做練習，請先把下列的英文複合形容詞譯成中文，再試著將一些常見的中文語彙轉換為英文。加油！

3-1. 請將下列英文翻成中文

heavy-handed ＿＿＿＿＿　　blue-eyed ＿＿＿＿＿

four-star ＿＿＿＿＿　　　　yellow-bellied ＿＿＿＿＿

3-2. 請將下列中文翻成英文

金髮的 ＿＿＿＿＿　　心腸好的 ＿＿＿＿＿

第一等的 ＿＿＿＿＿　　鬍子刮乾淨的 ＿＿＿＿＿

（4）have one's eye on sb/sth 特別留意；監視

build（指身材）（6 段）

They had their eye on me—that was why the man had come to make sure I was built tough enough.

他們看中了我，怪不得那位先生要親自檢查我的體格夠不夠強壯。

解析

此片語通常用在類似下列例句的情境：

◇ 你最好不要再偷錢了！我會一直盯著你。（註：在口語中，通常會用 have got 來表示 have）

You'd better not steal any more money! I've got my eye on you.

除了監視或注意他人，對某人有興趣時也可以用此片語，例如球探挖掘有潛力新人或故事中那位營造商那樣。have one's eye on sb/sth 堪稱為好用又好記的片語。

built 為此句另一重點，誠如大家所知，built 的原形動詞為 build，常指「建

造、蓋」，用以修飾人工打造的事物，例如房屋。不過人類也可以被「創造、塑造」出來，例如 built by God（上帝造人）、built by what they eat（人如其食）或 built by the circumstances they grow up in（由生長環境塑造而成）等，端看你怎麼想。當我們談論某人的 build 或 how someone be built，都是在談論「身材、體格」。像是可以用 stocky or slight（粗壯或瘦小）、straight or crooked（抬頭挺胸或彎腰駝背）或 weak or strong（體弱或強健）來形容身材。你會如何形容自己的身材呢？

小試身手

4-1. 他頸部厚實、胸膛寬闊，身材像拳擊手一樣好。

_____

4-2. 我留意她已經很久了，我想我會請她和我約會。

_____

（5）jump at the chance to... 非常高興地把握（難得的）機會（6 段）

Of course, I jumped at the chance to work in the city.
我當然立刻答應去城裡工作。

解析

有沒有哪個地方是你一直夢想要去的呢？有沒有那種工作是你夢寐以求的呢？絕大多數人都會點頭稱是。如果你突然有機會得以去參觀那個夢想之地或得到那份理想的工作，是不是會激動不已？你不只會得到實質好處，還會興奮到 jump for joy（雀躍不已）。這就是 jump at the chance to... 的由來，不會太難聯想，對吧？

小試身手

5. 我一直想去非洲旅行，所以我非常高興地把握能在那兒教英文的機會。

_____

(6) have no idea 根本不知道 (7 段)

At the time, I had no idea what he meant.
我當時不懂這是什麼意思。

解析

大家一定知道 idea 意指「主意」或「想法」。在漫畫或卡通中，當某人想到了一個主意，頭上常會出現一個電燈泡。但當燈泡總是不亮的時候會怎樣呢？那就代表你身陷黑暗當中，絲毫不知道該怎麼辦。

而 I have no idea.(我根本不知道)的語氣比 I don't know.(我不知道)強烈。這個句子夠簡單了吧，相信你一定看過，have no idea 可謂是英文中最常聽到和好用的實用片語之一，建議多用多說。

小試身手

6-1. 總統一點也不知道如何把經濟搞好。

_____

6-2. 他們根本不曉得怎麼處理全球暖化的問題。

_____

6-3. 我根本不知道他喜不喜歡你。

_____

（7）lack of... 缺乏……（11 段）

I really wanted to play around with the computer, but my lack of schooling made that impossible.

我很想玩這部電腦，可是我沒有念過書，不可能用電腦的。

解析

lack 意指「缺少、缺乏」，可用 lack of N. 來表示「缺乏(某物)，(某物)的不足」。一開始學到此片語時也許會覺得奇怪，因為中文的「缺乏」總是當作動詞，而非名詞。舉例來說，把 my lack of schooling 譯成中文時是「我缺乏教育」，而不是「我教育上的缺乏」。不過 lack of 在英文中仍被歸類為名詞片語就是了。茲舉兩例說明：

◇ 由於缺乏資金／資金不足，我們得要取消此研究計畫。
   Because of a lack of funding, we had to cancel the research project.
◇ 太魯閣國家公園不乏美景。
   There is no lack of beautiful scenery in Taroko National Park.

為了不讓大家因為 lack of practice(缺乏練習)而忘了這個片語，以下有三個句子請各位翻譯。祝大家好運！

小試身手

7-1. 他苦於缺乏社交的技巧。

_____

7-2. 我沒辦法不注意到她對我的不尊重。

_____

7-. 他們的失敗並非因為缺乏努力。

_____

(8) take sb. a while 花(某人)一段時間(12 段)

It took me quite a while to figure out what exactly a bank was.

我搞了半天，才弄懂了什麼叫銀行。

解析

句中的 take 意指「花(時間)」，而 while 可解釋為「一段時間」，quite 在此作副詞用，強調「很長的一段時間」，而 quite a while 亦可寫作 a long while 或 a long time，甚至是更不正式的 a good while。take 這個動詞通常(但非絕對)出現在虛主詞 it 後面，泛指「需要」，例如：

◇ 誰都可以寫歌，但是創作交響樂則需要真正的作曲家。
Anyone can write a song, but it takes a real composer to write a symphony.

◇ 要在商場上成功需要有腦袋。
To succeed in business takes brains.(It takes brains to succeed in business.)

小試身手

8-1. 你已經上網(好)一會兒了。你不覺得現在是寫功課的時間嗎？

_____

8-2. 我刷牙需要兩分鐘。

_____

8-3. 希拉蕊　柯林頓曾說：「養一個小孩需要全村的力量。」

_____

（9） make sure 確定；刻意做（12 段）

I had made sure to wear my best clothes to the bank.
我為了到銀行去，還刻意穿了最好的衣服。

解析

請將片語中 make 想成「使……變得」，而 sure 則想成「確定」。make sure of something 用於描述「額外關注某事物」、「對某事物付出更多的時間」等情境。make sure 後面可接 that 子句，而 that 通常予以省略，例如：

◇ 海倫，去確認客廳的燈是關著的。
   Helen, make sure the living room light is off.

◇ 去面試一定要打扮得宜。
   Make sure you dress nicely for the interview.

當 make sure 用於祈使句時，如以上兩例，可代換為 be sure。

小試身手

9-1. 鎖車前，要先確定鑰匙不在車內。

_____

9-2. 她知道夏威夷常下雨，所以她刻意帶了把雨傘去旅行。

_____

（10） 被動動詞片語可以當名詞用（16 段）

Being suspected by the police that day really made me angry.
我被警察懷疑的那件事，令我當天氣憤不已。

解析

對文法專有名詞有所恐懼的人而言，此解析的標題看來或許很複雜，但別擔心，中文和英文一樣都有簡單道理可循，如果你不相信的話，請看以下例句：

◇ 沒有人喜歡被欺負。
　No one likes being picked on.

你或許已注意到 being picked on 作為動詞 likes 的受詞。然而故事中的被動動詞片語 being suspected 是主詞。此用法在中文相當少見，因為我們不會說「被懷疑讓我很生氣」，不過，仔細看來仍有幾分道理。

小試身手

10-1. 禮拜五晚上一個人孤孤單單的可不好玩。

_____

10-2. 領薪水是工作最好的部分。

_____

（11）get in a fight（or argument）over... 為了……打架（17 段）

One day, one of my good friends got in a fight with a guy on the street over some little disagreement.

有一次，我的一位好友忽然為了一點小事和街上的一名路人打了起來。

解析

get 是英文中變化最為多端的一個動詞，和 get 相關的片語可以花好幾頁來敘述，幸好這裡只須了解 get in a fight 的意思即可，常可解釋為「發生肢體衝突」，而 get in 後面還可銜接 arguments、trouble 或其他不好的事情。當然，你也可以直接用動詞 fight 來表示 get in a fight，或用 argue 來表示 get in an argument，但這樣聽起來較為單調乏味。順帶補充，請注意此片語的時態慣用過去式，絕對不可能聽到英語母語人士說出 They're going to get in a fight tomorrow. 這樣的句子。

人們爭吵的理由百百種，所以介系詞 over 在此片語中扮演相當重要的角色，其後的受詞說明「爭吵的原因」，例如：

◇ 為了該由誰來清理烤箱，比利和他妹妹吵了起來。
Billy got in a fight with his sister over who should have to clean the oven.

很難解釋為什麼用 over，而不是 about，我認為是語言習慣的關係。小至夫妻意見不合、大至兩國開戰，各種爭吵相關片語的介系詞都是 over，例如：

◇ 各國為了如石油或土地等重要資源而開戰。
Countries fight over big things like oil and land.

◇ 人們會了金錢、嫉妒等小事而爭吵。
People get in fights over little things like money and jealousy.

小試身手

11-1. 你為什麼要為了這麼蠢的事打架？

_____

11-2. 兩個兄弟為了爭奪最後一塊蛋糕而打架。

_____

11-3. 我們為了該怎麼花這筆錢而起了爭執。

_____

(12) hold back 往後面拉（免得某事發生）(17 段)

He was lucky that we held him back—otherwise he might have hurt the guy.
還好被我們拉開，否則對方真可能被他打傷。

解析

hold 是「抓在手裡」，back 意指「向後、往後」，因此 hold back 在此顧名思義即指「(用手)往後拉」。不過，此片語還有其他意思，例如：

◇ 他因為期末考不及格，被留級而必須重讀三年級。（作「無法升級」解）
Because he didn't pass his final exams, he was held back and had to repeat the third grade.

◇ 你一直阻礙著我——為什麼你不讓我追求我的夢想？（作「阻礙」解）
You're always holding me back—why won't you let me follow my dreams?

◇ 她試圖忍住不哭，但還是掉淚了。（作「抑制」解）
She tried to hold back her tears, but they came anyway.

小試身手

12-1. 我覺得她的環境阻礙她——要是處境不同，她一定成就非凡。

_____

12-2. 那座水壩擋住了整個水庫的水。

_____

（13）be caught up in... 沈迷於……（17 段）

Caught up in the moment, he completely disregarded the risk that he'd be caught by the police.

就算可能會被警察抓，他當時已經管不了了。

解析

想到此片語時，請記住 catch 有「抓」的意思。你曾做過有趣到讓你渾然忘我的事情嗎？這種情況即可用 be caught up in... 來表示，就像被龍捲風捲離地面，必須等到回到地面(現實)才能開始做別的事。

故事中主人翁的朋友短暫耽溺於打架的快感，而忽略了後果。以下是 be caught up in... 的另一個例子：

◇ 我們太過沈迷於聊天，以致於完全忘了時間。
  We were so caught up in our conversation that we completely forgot about the time.

> **小試身手**
>
> 13-1. 我沒有聽到電話鈴聲，因為我太專心聽我的音樂了。
>
> _____
>
> 13-2. 她沈迷於開新車的快感，根本忘了速限。
>
> _____

（14）take out（anger）on... 發洩（怒氣）在……身上（18 段）

Strange to say, I took out all my anger on the steel—working alone, I bent dozens of rods in just two hours.

說也奇怪，我將我的一股怨氣，完全發洩在鋼筋上，幾十條鋼筋，我一個人兩小時就全部弄彎了。

解析

除了極少數修為極高的人，一般人大多會感到生氣或懊惱。有人會將挫折、失意都往肚裡吞，直到承受不了時才瞬間爆發；有些人則藉由運動或跟朋友抱怨來抒發情緒；也有人會把氣出在無辜的人身上或摔東西。故事中的主角則屬第三種。英文中用 take out anger on sb./sth. 來表示「把怒氣發洩在某人或事物身上」，有人或許會質疑為何用 take 這麼溫和的字，而不是 blow 或 attack 等語氣較為強烈的字眼，但慣用語就是如此，千萬別自作聰明擅加改變。想到此片語時，可以想像一下有人把體內累積已久的怒氣 take out（拿出來）。有一點須注意，take out 的受詞多半會用 it 來代指 anger。

小試身手

27. 我知道你生氣了，可是不要發洩在我身上。

_____

（15）hang out 玩；混

Not long after that, I started hanging out with the train surfers.
不久，我參加了火車的飆車族。

解析

小孩子一起玩，可以用 play with each other 來表示，但是想要形容青少年或成人聚在一起玩樂、閒晃、打發時間，就必須用 hang out，例如：

◇ 克拉拉和她的朋友喜歡在購物中心裡頭閒晃。
　 Clara and her friends like to hang out at the mall.

◇ 布萊德有時會跟艾瑞克一起玩，但絕不會跟約伯。
　 Brad sometimes hangs out with Eric, but never with Jacob.

須注意第一個例句重點是在「哪裡」閒晃，而第二句的重點在於跟「誰」一起玩，事實上，一個人也可以 hang out，例如：I'm just hanging out at home, watching TV.（我待在家裡看電視打發時間。）

雖然 hang out 的意思很多,但要小心有些情況下會有截然不同的意思,例如 Freshly washed clothes can be hung out to dry.(可以把剛洗好的衣物吊在外面晾乾),而 let it all hang out 意指「全裸」或「全盤托出、毫無隱瞞」之意。通常,可從上下文判別其義。

小試身手

15-1. 我覺得她交錯朋友了。

_____

15-2. A:我會遲到一下。

　　　B:沒關係,我會在這裡閒晃等你來。

_____

_____

---

(16) move up to... 進步到⋯⋯(22 段)

After surfing the slow trains for a while, some of us moved up to the fast ones.

飆完慢車以後,有人就會進步到飆快車。

解析

把飆車速度和考試成績兩相比擬時,飆慢車就像考低分,飆快車就像考高分。只有最好的學生可以 move up to(進步到)得高分。藉由這個例子,大家可以了解 move up to 是 be promoted to 或 progress to 的非正式用法。你也會注意到此用法並非全然用在好的一面——飆快車顯然是不好的。一個明顯的例子即罪犯一開始所犯罪行皆屬小奸小惡,不過小惡做多了,很快就會「發展成」move up to 大惡。

16. 有了這份高薪的新差事，她就能從本田升級到保時捷。

_____

(17) ...of (them) all 最……(23 段)

Then one day, I met the gutsiest train surfer of all.
有一次，我發現一位非常勇敢的飆車手。

解析

舉例來說，公司裡的張三和李四因為過人的聰明才智而引人注目，但老王才全公司最聰明的那一位，當你想要強調某人在一個大型團體中是「最……的」，就可用 of all 形容之。例如，在《白雪公主》童話中，邪惡皇后所問的 "Mirror, mirror on the wall, who's the fairest of them all?" (「魔鏡啊魔鏡，誰是世界上最美的女人呢？」)，最後一句的含意即 who's the most beautiful woman in the world?，又如一首著名聖誕歌曲的歌名所示 "Do you recall the most famous reindeer of all?" (你記得最有名的馴鹿是哪一隻嗎？)。另外要請大家注意，只有在 most 後面接形容詞，而非名詞時，them 才會出現在 of 和 all 之間，亦即 most + adj. + of them all。

17-1. 我曾被朋友背叛過，但你的背叛讓我最感痛苦。

_____

17-2. 所有運動員都很強悍，但他是其中最強悍的。

_____

（18）catch sb's eye 引起某人的注意（25 段）

Being a young man, I caught the eye of a white-haired old priest when I went in to pray.

我這個年輕人進來祈禱，引起一位白髮蒼蒼的老神父的注意。

解析

欲理解此片語，可先想想 catch 的意思。你會 catch（接住）投向你的球。警方 catch（逮捕）逃跑的罪犯。在這兩種情況中，catch 都可解釋為「抓住」之意。而 eye 除了表示身體器官的「眼睛」之外，亦指「眼光」或「注意」，不管是主動還是被動，任何事物引起你的注意時，都可用 catch sb's eye。能引起注意的東西可用形容詞 eye-catching 來表示。（請參閱解析3「用連字號創造的複合形容詞」用法）

小試身手

18-1. 窗邊的紫光引起了我的注意。

_____

18-2. 她往他的方向一看，試著引起他的注意。

_____

（19）in the distance 在遠處（27 段）

The train has just appeared in the distance.

火車已在遠處出現。

解析

一看到 distance，你可能會馬上聯想到「距離」，不過如果你只知道這個意思的話，in the distance 在文中的意思就說不通了。身為敏銳讀者，你必須根據上下文來判斷出正確的意思，並從而得出 in the distance 等同於 far away，也就是「在遠處(方)、離……很遠的地方」，當你遇到一個片語拆開每個單字都認識，但組合在一起意思卻和字面上差很多時，可以發揮「猜」功，從上下文去找出正確解釋。

小試身手

19. 黑煙從遠方工廠緩緩升起。

_____

小試身手解答

1.　I was born and raised in the central mountains of Taiwan.

2-1.　Since we're going to stay here for a while, why did you leave the engine running?

2-2.　Highway 7 runs/passes through many high mountains.

2-3.　She's a wanderer, always passing through, never staying.
　　　(須注意，此句的 run through 不可代換為 pass through)

3-1.　手法太重的或笨手笨腳的　　　藍眼的

　　　四星的　　　　　　　　　　懦弱的

3-2.　blonde-haired　　　　　　　kind-hearted

　　　first-rate 或 first-class　　clean-shaven

4-1.　With a thick neck and a massive chest, he was built like a boxer.

4-2.　I've had my eye on her for a while now; I think I'll ask her on a date.

5.　I had always wanted to travel to Africa, so I jumped at the chance to teach English there.

6-1.　The president has no idea how to fix the economy.

6-2.　They have no idea how to deal with (the problem of) global warming.

6-3.　I have no idea if he likes you (or not).

7-1.　He suffers from a lack of social skills.

7-2. I could not help but notice her lack of respect for me.

7-3. Their failure wasn't due to (a) lack of effort.

8-1. You've been on the Internet for (quite) a while　Don't you think it's time (that) you did your homework?

8-2. It takes me two minutes to brush my teeth.

8-3. Hillary Clinton once said, "It takes a village to raise a child."

9-1. Before you lock the car, make sure the keys aren't inside.
（可代換為 be sure）

9-2. She knew it rained a lot in Hawaii, so she made sure to bring an umbrella on her trip. （不可代換為 be sure）

10-1. Being alone on a Friday night is no fun.

10-2. The best part of work is getting paid.
（註：你可以用 being paid 來代替 getting paid，不過 getting paid 較不正式，用在此句較為恰當。同樣地，Being paid is the best part of work.在文法上正確，但是聽起來怪怪的）

11-1. Why would you get in a fight over something so silly?

11-2. The two brothers fought over the last piece of cake.
（此句不宜使用 get in fight，因為他們不是真的毆打對方。）

11-3. We got in an argument over how we should spend the money.

12-1. I think her environment holds her back—if her circumstances were different, she would excel.

12-2. That dam holds back an entire reservoir of water.

13-1. I didn't hear the phone ring because I was too caught up in my music.

13-2. Caught up in the thrill of driving a new car, she completely forgot about the speed limit.

14.　I know you're angry, but don't take it out on me.

15-1. I think she hangs out with the wrong kind of people.

15-2. A: I'm going to be a little late.

　　　B: That's OK, I'll just hang out here until you come.

16.　With her high-paying new job, she could afford to move up from a Honda to a Porsche.

17-1. I have been betrayed by friends before, but yours is the most painful betrayal of all.

17-2. All athletes are tough, but he's the toughest of them all.

18-1. The purple light in the window caught my eye.

18-2. She glanced his way, trying to catch his eye.

19.　Black smoke rose slowly from the factory in the distance.

Deep River
—Shusaku Endo's Masterpiece

《深河》
——遠藤周作的鉅作

1-5　　　我一直喜歡看遠藤周作的小說，這位聞名世界的日本作家，寫的小說都平易近人，沒有什麼看不懂的地方。遠藤周作最近完成一本小說，英文名稱是 "Deep River" 中文譯名為《深河》。

　　上個月，我到澳洲墨爾本出差，路過一家天主教書店，一進去就買到了這本書，在旅館反正沒事可做，當天晚上就開始看。

　　所謂《深河》，指的是印度的恆河，故事是有關一個日本的旅行團，到印度去觀光。其中一位女士，曾經在大學時認識過一位男同學，這位男同學做了天主教神父，也去了印度，於是乎這位女士就到印度來找尋她當年心儀的男孩子。

　　可是她卻老是找不到他，有些天主教堂裡的神職人員顯然知道他在那裡，可是就是不肯講，好像不屑談論這位神父，也有點暗示他早已離開教會。

　　其實他依然是位神父，只是他不住在教堂裡，卻住在加爾各答最貧窮的地區，附近住的全是印度階級制度下的賤民。這位女士去拜訪他的時候，他不在家，而她卻被當地的窮困景像嚇壞了。留下了旅館的電話，匆匆離去。

CD2-2
- overly (adv.) 過於
- involve (v.) 牽涉到；和……有關
- terribly (adv.) 非常
- clergyman (n.) 神職人員
- whereabouts (n.) 行蹤；下落
- disdain (v.) 不屑；鄙視
- imply (v.) 暗示

I have always enjoyed reading the novels of Shusaku Endo, the world-famous Japanese author. The books he writes are easy to understand, without any overly difficult passages. Endo's last novel is titled *Deep River* in English, or《深河》in the Chinese translation.

1-5
CD2-1

Last month, during a business trip to Melbourne, Australia, I happened upon a Catholic bookstore; I walked right in and bought the book. Since I had nothing to do in my hotel, I went ahead and started reading it that night.

The river referred to by the title is the Ganges of India. The story involves a group of Japanese tourists who travel to India. One of them, a woman, has come to look for an old college classmate she admired who became a Catholic priest and left to serve in India.

She has a terribly difficult time finding him, however. Several clergymen obviously know his whereabouts, but they refuse to tell her. They seem to disdain to talk about this priest and imply that he has left the church.

It turns out that he is still a priest, only he does not live in a chapel—he lives in the poorest part of Calcutta, surrounded by the "untouchables" at the bottom of the Hindu caste system. When the woman goes to visit him, he is not at home. Frightened by the wretched poverty she sees there, she leaves the telephone number of her hotel and hurries away.

◇ untouchables (n.) 賤民(印度最低階層的人民)
◇ Hindu (adj.) 印度(教)的
◇ wretched (adj.) 悲慘的；可憐的
◇ poverty (n.) 貧窮；貧困(形容詞 poor 的名詞形式)

　　神父的電話來了，他問那位女士住那一家旅館，當他知道是一間豪華的觀光旅館以後，就告訴她，他現在衣衫襤褸，和一般賤民一模一樣，所以旅館警衛不會讓他進去的，最後他們約定在旅館外面的一張長椅上見面。

6-10

　　這位神父究竟在做什麼呢？他平時一早起來，做彌撒、祈禱，和別的神父一樣，可是他主要的工作就和別人完全不一樣了。對於印度教信徒而言，恆河是一條特別的河流，絕大多數的印度人都想要去恆河沐浴一次，如此對他們的靈魂有很大的好處。對有錢人，這件事不難，可是對於一些貧無立錐之地的窮人，他們必須步行到恆河去，很多人到了加爾各答，因為旅途勞頓而再也到不了恆河。

　　我們的神父發現了這種人以後，會問他是否要去恆河，如果是的話，神父會將他背到恆河去。

　　其實這個故事有其象徵性的意義，恆河代表上蒼無盡的愛，富人和窮人，他們的骨灰，都進入了恆河，正如上蒼一樣，上蒼接受富人，更接受窮人，而這位神父所做的，卻又是耶穌基督生平的重演，遠藤周作在另一篇小說中，特別形容耶穌生命中的最後一刻，在那篇小說中，耶穌懇求人家，讓他背沉重的十字架，因為他要背負全人類的痛

◇ luxurious (adj.) 豪華的 (luxury 的形容詞形式)
◇ rags (n.) 破爛的衣服 (常用複數形，單數名詞 rag 意為「破布」)

◇ outcaste (n.)（印度）被剝奪種姓的人；賤民
◇ aspire (v.) 嚮往

The priest calls her and asks what hotel she is staying in. When he learns that it is a luxurious tourist hotel, he informs her that because he now dresses in rags like the outcastes around him, the guards at the hotel will not let him enter. Eventually they arrange to meet on a bench outside the hotel.

So what exactly does the priest do? Usually he rises early in the morning, performs mass and prays, just like any other priest. But his most important work is completely unique. To Hindus, the Ganges is a special river. The vast majority of Indians aspire to bathe in it at least once, for they believe that this will greatly benefit their souls. For the rich, this is not difficult to accomplish, but many of the desperately poor must make the journey on foot, and some of them arrive in Calcutta so road-weary that they are unable to reach the river.

6-10

Whenever our priest finds these people, he asks them if they are traveling to the Ganges; if they are, he carries them there on his back.

There is much symbolism embedded in the story. The Ganges represents God's infinite love. The ashes of rich and poor alike find their final resting place there—like God, the Ganges accepts them both. And what the priest does is a reenactment of the life of Jesus Christ. In another novel, Shusaku Endo describes the last moments of Jesus' life: Jesus asks to bear a man's heavy cross, for he himself

- bathe [beð] (v.) 沐浴（注意發音和 bath [bæθ] 不同）
- accomplish (v.) 成就；實現
- desperately (adv.) 極度地(desperate
- 意為走投無路的)
- embed (v.) 把……嵌進
- reenactment (n.) 重演
- bear (v.) 背負

苦。這位神父之所以背一位窮人去恆河，無非是要表明一件事：基督徒應該背耶穌給我們的十字架，替窮人服務，更應該帶領人們到達永生，恆河對於印度人而言，代表永生也。

一位神父背著一位異教徒，去完成這位異教徒的心願，是否有點奇怪？關於這點，我想起了德蕾莎修女的垂死之家，在這座垂死之家，有一間停屍間，停屍間左排標明佛教徒，右排標明印度教，而停屍間的門上有一排字「去見耶穌的路上」。

遠藤周作顯然對德蕾莎修女的印象極深，他所形容的那位神父，其所做所為也極像德蕾莎修女，他們都不是光靠一張嘴來傳播福音，他們以行動來表示他們是基督徒。

11-15　　第二天，我從一所大學訪問回來，由於是正式訪問，我穿得西裝筆挺，回旅館的時候，門口的警衛對我微微欠身，而且打開門讓我進去，我走進了大廳，大廳裡兩邊都是落地的大鏡子。從鏡子裡，我可以看到我自己神氣活現的嘴臉，我忽然想起《深河》裡的那位神父，他不敢走進豪華的旅館，因為他衣衫襤褸，人家一定看不起他。

◇ immortality (n.) 不死；永生
◇ pagan (n.)(基督徒眼中的)異教徒
◇ fulfill (v.) 完成
◇ ponder (v.) 思索

◇ morgue (n.) 停屍間
◇ tremendous (adj.) 巨大的
◇ solely (adv.) 僅僅
◇ slightly (adv.) 稍微

must bear the pains of all mankind. By bearing a poor man or woman to the Ganges, the priest affirms that a Christian ought to take up the cross Christ gave us, serve the poor, and lead people to eternal life. To Indians, the Ganges represents immortality.

Is it not a bit strange for a priest to carry a pagan on his back to fulfill that pagan's dying wish? While pondering this, I recalled that in Mother Teresa's Home for the Dying, there was a morgue with the row on the left marked "Buddhist" and the row on the right marked "Hindu," and the words "On the way to meet Jesus" written above the door.

Obviously Mother Teresa made a tremendous impression on Shusaku Endo. The priest he describes is very like her in that neither of them relies solely on words to preach the gospel: they express their Christianity through action.

The following day, I returned from a visit to a university. Because it was a formal visit, I wore a freshly pressed suit. When I returned to my hotel, the guard bowed slightly toward me and opened the door for me to enter. I walked into the lobby, which was lined on both sides with floor-length mirrors in which I could see the reflection of my self-satisfied smirk. Suddenly I thought of the priest in *Deep River*, who dared not walk into a luxury hotel for fear that his ragged clothes would draw looks of contempt.

11-15

◇ reflection (n.) 映像
◇ smirk (n.)（自以為了不起或用以嘲笑別人的）笑
◇ ragged (adj.) 破爛的；衣衫襤褸的
◇ contempt (n.) 蔑視

　　而我呢？我現在神氣活現地進入旅館，如果有一天，我一命嗚乎，要到天堂去報到(如果有此資格的話)，我一定羞愧得要在天堂門口躲躲閃閃，到那時，我一定會說，「我衣衫襤褸，身無分文，天堂裡的人不會歡迎我的」。反過來說，我相信，那位神父死去以後，天堂的守門人一定會對他鞠躬，打開大門讓他進去。我這種人呢？能混進去就已經很高興的了。

　　遠藤周作的《深河》替基督教義做了最佳的詮釋，有些這類的書，多多少少會冒犯了不信基督教的人，可是，這本書絕對不會，任何人看了這本書，都會知道，所謂「基督徒」該是什麼樣的人。

　　《深河》已拍成了電影，據說頗受年輕人歡迎。對於我這個老年人，我常常在想，希望有一天，我不敢堂而皇之地到大旅館去，也不敢神氣活現地和大人物來往，到那時候，我才敢抬起頭來，勇敢地面對上蒼。

　　我該感謝《深河》給我的啟示。

◇ gasp (v.) 喘
◇ linger (v.) 徘徊；逗留
◇ ashamed (adj.) 慚愧的；羞恥的(名詞 shame 的形容詞形式)
◇ thrilled (adj.) 非常興奮的
◇ present (v.) 呈現

And me? I had strode proudly into the hotel as if I owned the place. But if, one day, I gasp my last breath and report in to heaven (if I am qualified to go there), surely I will linger uncomfortably at the gate, ashamed to go in. Then I will say, "My clothes are ragged and I am penniless; they won't welcome me in heaven." On the other hand, I believe that when that priest dies, the heavenly gatekeeper will bow to him and open the gate to let him through. But a man like me would be thrilled to get in any way he could.

Shusaku Endo's *Deep River* presents Christian doctrine in the best possible light. Some books in the genre tend to offend non-Christians to some degree, but this book absolutely does not. Anyone who reads it will know what manner of person a Christian ought to be.

Deep River has been made into a movie, which I hear is quite popular among young people. Being an older man, I often ponder: hopefully there will come a day when I dare not stride confidently into a big hotel or take pompous pleasure in associating with the high and mighty. Only at that day will I be able to hold my head high and face God courageously.

I am grateful for the inspiration *Deep River* has given me.

◇ doctrine (n.) 教義；原理
◇ genre (n.) (文學、電影等的)類型
◇ offend (v.) 得罪
◇ pompous (adj.) 自以為是的
◇ associate with (v.) 和……來往
◇ inspiration (n.) 啟發；靈感

（1） happen upon/on... 偶然遇到；偶然找到（物或地方）（1 段）

Last month, during a business trip to Melbourne, Australia, I happened upon a Catholic bookstore…

上個月，我到澳洲墨爾本出差，路過一家天主教書店。

【解析】

想理解這個片語，要先記得：事情不全是如你預期般的發生。俗話說，踏破鐵鞋無覓處，得來全不費工夫，有時候你得找出你需要的，但有時候你剛好就遇到你需要的。例如：

◇ 當我走過城區，我路過一家很棒的小壽司店。
　 While I was walking through town, I happened upon this great little sushi restaurant.

◇ 一天，當我在打掃閣樓時，我剛好發現一盒爺爺的舊照片。
　 One day, as I was cleaning the attic, I happened on a box of grandpa's old photos.

┌───┐
│ 小試身手   │
│   │
│ 1-1. 正在我開始覺得迷路的時候，剛好走到一個地鐵站。   │
│   │
│ _____ │
│   │
│ 1-2. 為什麼你要求不要在披薩上放橄欖？我偏偏(剛好)喜歡橄欖耶！ │
│   │
│ _____ │
└───┘

（2） go ahead and... 就先……（1 段）

Since I had nothing to do in my hotel, I went ahead and started reading it that night.

在旅館反正沒事可做，當天晚上就開始看。

[解析]

go ahead 帶有一種積極進取的味道，所以不要用在「不得已」的情況，因為它只用在自發的情境。例如說，你跟兩個朋友在餐廳一起等著遲到的另一位友人，或許你可以不等他來就先點餐 (You can go ahead and order without him if you want.)；抑或是你是個表現傑出的學生，一旦你做完這星期的功課還有多餘時間的話，你就可以先看下週的閱讀教材 (You might go ahead and do your reading for next week once you finish your assignments for this week.)。

注意，go ahead 也可以只表示字面上的意義「走在前面」。如果你跟朋友一起爬山，你喘不過氣來，需要休息一下，這時候你就可以說："You go (on) ahead—I'll catch up in a minute."

小試身手

2-1. 你們何不先開始吃？不用等我。

_____

2-2. 我事先就買好一條項鍊當禮物了，儘管她的生日要下個月才會到。

_____

(3) refer to... 指……（2 段）

The river referred to by the title is the Ganges of India.
所謂《深河》，指的是印度的恆河。

[解析]

世界上有許多深河：長江、亞瑪遜河、窩瓦河、多瑙河和尼羅河等等。如何表達題目說的「深河」？ refer to 即為「指的是」，例如：

◇ 我有兩個叫 Jack 的朋友，你指的是哪一個？
I have two friends named Jack—which one are you referring to?

◇ 通常，當他談論政客時，他指的是他不喜歡的那些人。
Usually, when he talks about politicians, he's referring to the ones he doesn't like.

這是一個很有用的片語，口語和書寫都很常用，用起來感覺英語更道地。試試看！

小試身手

3-1. 在中國，「抗戰」指的是第二次世界大戰。

_____

3-2. 他指的是哪個計畫——我的還是他的？

_____

（4）it turns out that... 原來……（4 段）

It turns out that he is still a priest.
其實他依然是神父。

解析

雖然原文並無「原來」二字，但要譯出 "it turns out that..." 就須加個「原來」來順順語氣。 "it turns out that..." 常用在說故事，通常強調期望和真實之間的不同，或是傳達驚訝的感覺。文中的另一個神父曾暗示女士，她的朋友已離開天主教堂，所以她對於她朋友仍然是牧師這件事，可能會有些驚訝。 "turn out" 可以大略翻譯成「原來是……(happens afterward)」，有了 "happen" 這個字，就帶了點不確定的意味(如同解析一)，如果這段的解釋看起來有點複雜，看看下面的例子就會比較明白。

◇ 當我知道他是獨生子時，我不懂他為何老是提起他哥哥。原來他指的是他同母異父的兄弟。

I couldn't figure out why he always talked about his brother when I knew he is an only child. It turned out that he was referring to his half-brother.

◇ 原來公司數年來都在虧損──到現在他們對此事一直都在說謊。

Turns out the company has been losing money for years—they've just been lying about it until now.

小試身手

4-1. 原來學英文可以很好玩，只要用正面的態度學。

_____

4-2. 許多人以為豬很笨，但實際上豬是相當聰明的動物。

_____

小小變化

5-3.「他」原來是個打扮得像男生的女生。

_____

（5）What exactly... 究竟什麼……？（6 段）

So what exactly does the priest do?

這位神父究竟在做什麼呢？

解析

"exactly" 這個字增加了整個片語的準確度。「一百元」和「一百元整」有些微的不同：前者可能是大約，後者卻是一個精確的量。"exactly" 還可以

強調某件事實，例如你跟朋友在聊老闆超愛自我吹噓，突然，你的老闆馬上就在吹噓他的賓士。他走後，你就可對朋友說： "See? That's exactly what I mean!"

在本文中，exactly 被譯成「究竟」。其實中文的「究竟」並沒有相對應的英文，但通常可以用 exactly 來表達出大概的意思。exactly 表示詢問者有相當程度的好奇，並希望聽到更多細節的回答。

小試身手

5-1. 我在那家店正好花了五十美元。

_____

5-2. 你要表達的究竟是什麼？

_____

（6）is it not... 不是……嗎？（9 段）

Is it not a bit strange for a priest to carry a pagan on his back to fulfill that pagan's dying wish?
一位神父背著一位異教徒，去完成這位異教徒的心願，是否有點奇怪？

解析

這裡是一個很好的反問句（只是為了行文的效果，而非要對方真的回答）。

◇ 我反對增加房產稅。我們已經付了30%的所得稅難道還不夠嗎？
I oppose raising property taxes. Is it not enough that we already pay a 30% income tax?

你可以用名字或代名詞來取代 it，也可以把 is...not 縮寫成 isn't ，讓文章感覺更隨意。如同下面例句一樣：

◇ 那寶寶好可愛不是嗎？
Isn't that a cute baby?

◇ 約翰可不是你遇過最好的傢伙？
Isn't John the nicest guy you've ever met?

小試身手

6-1. 那豈不是個很糟糕的主意？

_____

6-2. 他們才交往兩個月，現在談婚姻是否有點太快？

_____

---

7. in that... 從以下的角度來看 (10 段)

The priest he describes is very like her in that neither of them relies solely on words to preach the gospel.

他所形容的那位神父，其所做所為也極像德蕾莎修女，他們都不是光靠一張嘴傳播福音。

解析

如同解析5的 exactly，這是加強句子細節的另一種說法。沒錯，他們兩個都是天主教徒，他們也都侍奉窮人，但這不是李教授在這裡想說的。他要說的是，他們在某個特定之處的相像：他們用行動而非言語，來傳達他們的信仰。以下為 in that 的兩個例子：

◇ 她的特出之處，在於當她錯的時候，她願意承認。("in that" 後面解釋她為何獨特的原因)
She is unique in that she is willing to admit when she's wrong.

◇ 我們向來的敗筆在於一直忽視窮人。
We have failed in that we continue to neglect the poor.

本句的 like 是「像」的意思。可以加 very 在前，例如： That sofa is very like my own. (那沙發跟我的很像。)這的用法相當不正式，但在文法上是對的。但是如果 like 當動詞，做「喜歡」解釋時，前面當然就不能加 very。

小試身手

7-1. 我覺得所有的小鎮都大同小異。(一個小鎮和另一個小鎮差不多。)

_____

7-2. 他常捐錢給慈善團體，在這方面他是很大方的。

_____

(8) self-satisfied 自滿；自以為了不起(11 段)

I could see the reflection of my self-satisfied smirk.

從鏡子裡，我可以看到我自己神氣活現的嘴臉。

解析

這個詞顯然帶有貶意。聽起來可能有點怪，因為通常「滿足」沒啥不好的——事實上，幸福的祕訣就在於滿足於你所擁有的。但「自滿」就是另一回事囉！那表示你對自己很滿意，甚至比其他人都要好。換句話說，那表示你自負自誇，可是卻沒人會喜歡臭屁的人。smirk 是個貶意字(pejorative)，帶著一點嘲諷挖苦的微笑或自滿到不行的表情。總之，self-satisfied 就表達了「神氣活現的嘴臉」的意思。

小試身手

8. 無論你多聰明，你絕不應該自以為了不起。

_____

（9）for fear that... （因為）怕……（11 段）

Suddenly I thought of the priest in *Deep River*, who dared not walk into a luxury hotel for fear that his ragged clothes would draw looks of contempt.

我忽然想起《深河》裡的那位神父，他不敢走進豪華的旅館，因為他衣衫襤褸，人家一定看不起他。

解析

如解析10的 in that... ，這裡的 for fear that... 是另一個有用的片語，適用於放在句尾以解釋原因。

◇ 她反對較嚴格的習俗規範，因為她擔心這樣做的壞處多過於好處。
　 She opposes stricter customs regulations for fear that they will do more harm than good.

◇ 他拒絕在課堂上念自己的詩，免得被笑。
　 He refused to read his poetry in front of the class for fear of being laughed at.

在第二個例句裡，我們用 for fear of... ，而不是 for fear that... ，你知道為什麼嗎？那是因為 that 以後加子句，of 後面加名詞片語（N. / Ving），原理都是一樣的。

小試身手

9-1. 她迴避告訴他實話，因為怕他會心煩。

_____

9-2. 因為怕即將要來的颱風，我們取消了旅行的計畫。

_____

10. present sth. in adj. light 以……方式表達……（13段）

Shusaku Endo's *Deep River* presents Christian doctrine in the best possible light.

遠藤周作的《深河》替基督教義做了最佳的詮釋。

解析

每個研究劇場跟攝影的人一定都知道燈光的重要性。在典型的恐怖片中，壞蛋一定從底下打燈，讓他們看起來更邪惡。下次當你身處黑暗當中，你可以自己拿個手電筒從下往上照，看看自己有多恐怖！相反的，愉快的、明亮的燈光總會帶給人平靜和明朗的感覺。

寫作意念的表達和劇場並無二致：可用適切的燈光表現種種不同（present sth. in adj. light）。「信耶穌得永生，不信耶穌下地獄」表現了基督教義褊狹、唐突的一面，甚少有人會接受這樣的訊息，但強調愛、服務和忍耐，如同《深河》裡的牧師一樣，能讓基督教義得到更正面的理解。

小試身手

10-1. 如果你希望他們僱用你，你就得以討人喜歡的方式表現你自己。

_____

10-2. 讓我們換一個角度去看它。

_____

(11) anyone who... 任何……的人，都……（13 段）

Anyone who reads it will know what manner of person a Christian ought to be.

任何人看了這本書，都會知道，所謂「基督徒」該是什麼樣的人。

解析

學過英文的人都知道 anyone 是什麼意思，但你很少跟關係代名詞詞 who 連用吧？這邊的 who 是限定用法，讓我們知道所指的是那一種人。例如：

◇ 穿涼鞋又穿襪子的人不懂時尚。
Anyone who wears socks and sandals together doesn't understand fashion.

◇ 我尊重能維護自己信仰的人。
I respect anyone who stands up for what he believes in.

當然，其他由 any 衍生的代名詞，像 anything 和 anywhere，也可使用同樣原則，但跟在 any- 後面的片語是有限制性的。例如：

◇ 如果你看到特價的東西，就可以買。
If you see anything that's on sale, buy it.

◇ 我會帶你去任何你想去的地方。
I'll take you anywhere you want to go.

小試身手

11-1. 我不認識任何一個沒有聽過 Tom Cruise 的人。

_____

11-2. 你的命令是射任何移動的東西。

_____

11-3. Tyler 的任何一個朋友都是我的朋友。

_____

小試身手解答

1-1. Just as I began to feel lost, I happened on a subway station.

1-2. Why did you ask for no olives on the pizza? I happen to like olives!

2-1. Why don't you go ahead and start eating without me?

2-2. I went ahead and bought her the necklace as a gift, even though her birthday was not until next month.

3-1. In China, the "War of Resistance（against the Japanese）" refers to World War II.

3-2. Which plan is he referring to—his or mine?

4-1. [It] turns out [that] learning English can be a lot of fun, if you do it with a positive attitude.（"it" 和 "that" 在非正式用法中均可省略。）

4-2. Many people think pigs are stupid, but it turns out that they are actually quite intelligent animals.

4-3. "He" turned out to be a woman dressed like a man.

5-1. I spent exactly 50 dollars at the store.

5-2. What exactly is it that you're trying to say? 或 What exactly are you trying to say?

6-1. Isn't that a terrible idea?

6-2. They've only been together for two months—isn't it a little early to be talking about marriage?

7-1. In my opinion, one town is very like another.

7-2. He is generous in that he often donates money to charity.

8. No matter how smart you are, you should never become self-satisfied.

9-1. She avoided telling him the truth for fear that it would upset him.

9-2. We canceled our travel plans for fear of the incoming typhoon.

10-1. If you want them to hire you, you have to present yourself in a favorable light.

10-2. Let's look at it in a different light.

11-1. I don't know anyone who hasn't heard of Tom Cruise.

11-2. Your orders are to shoot anything that moves.

11-3. Any friend of Tyler's is a friend of mine.

The Porcelain Dolls
瓷娃娃

1-5

我在柏克萊念博士的時候，交到了一位美國好朋友，他叫約翰。我當時是單身漢，他已婚，太太非常和善。他們常邀我到他家吃飯，我有請必到，變成他們家經常的座上客。

約翰夫婦都是學生，當然收入不多，可是家裡卻佈置得舒適極了。他們會買便宜貨，收集了不少的瓷娃娃：有吹喇叭的小男孩，有打傘的小女孩，也有小男孩在摸狗等等的娃娃，滿屋子都是這種擺設，窗檯上更是放了一大排。我每次到他們家都會把玩這些瓷娃娃。

約翰告訴我他們的瓷娃娃都是從舊貨店和舊貨攤買來的。有一天，我發現一家舊貨店，也去買了一個瓷娃娃，是一個高高瘦瘦的少女，低著頭，一臉憂鬱的表情。等約翰夫婦再請我去的時候，我將它帶去，他們大為高興，告訴我這是西班牙 Lladró 娃娃，這家名牌公司的娃娃個個又高又瘦，也都帶著憂鬱的表情。他們一直想要有這麼一個娃娃，可是始終沒有找到，沒有想到我卻買到了。

◇ Ph.D. (n.) 博士學位（Doctor of Philosophy 的縮寫）
◇ regular (adj.) 經常的
◇ furnish (v.) 擺設
◇ accumulate (v.) 累積
◇ sizable (adj.) 可觀的
◇ collection (n.) 收藏品（動詞 collect 意為「收集」）
◇ pet (v.) 撫摸（寵物）
◇ decorate (v.) 布置；裝潢
◇ row (n.) 排
◇ windowsill (n.) 窗台

While studying for my Ph.D. at Berkeley, I became good friends with an American named John. I was single then, and he was married to a wonderful woman. The two of them often invited me over for meals. I accepted every invitation and soon became a regular guest in their home.

John and his wife were both students, so naturally they didn't make much money, but their home was quite comfortably furnished. They would buy things on sale, and they had accumulated a sizable collection of porcelain dolls: there was a boy blowing a horn, a girl holding an umbrella, a boy petting a dog and all sorts of others. The whole room was decorated with them—there was even a row of dolls on the windowsill. I would play around with them whenever I came over.

John told me that they had gotten their dolls from secondhand stores and street booths. One day I happened to pass by a secondhand store, so I bought a porcelain doll there. It was a tall, slender maiden looking down with a melancholy expression. The next time John and his wife invited me over, I brought it with me. They loved it. They told me it was a Lladró figurine from Spain—Lladró's famous figurines had a tendency to be tall, thin and melancholy-looking. They had always wanted a doll like that, but they had never seen one for sale. It surprised them that I had been able to buy one.

◇ booth (n.) 攤子
◇ slender (adj.) 苗條的
◇ maiden (n.) 少女；閨女
◇ melancholy (adj.) 憂鬱的
◇ figurine (n.) 小雕像
◇ tendency (n.) 傾向

　　我們先後拿到博士以後就各奔前程。約翰的研究是有關感測器，畢業後不久就自己開了一家公司，用感測器作一些防盜器材。他很快地大量使用電腦，生意也越來越大，還當上美國最大的保全系統公司的老闆。由於中東問題，美國飛機好幾次被恐怖分子所劫持，約翰的公司得了大的合約，替美國大的機場設計安全系統，大概畢業二十年以後，他的身價已是快四億美金。

　　有一年，我決定去找他，他欣然答應接待我，那時已近耶誕節，我先去他的辦公室，他親自帶我去看他的系統展覽室，我才知道現在的汽車防盜系統幾乎都是他們的產品，體積極小，孩子如果隨身攜帶，父母永遠可以知道他在那裡，我也發現美國很多監獄都由他們設計安全系統，以防止犯人逃脫。

6-10　　看完展覽以後，約翰開車和我一起到他家去。那一天天氣變壞了，天空飄雪。約翰的家在紐約州的鄉下，全是有錢人住的地方，當他指給我看他的住家時，我簡直以為我自己在看電影，如此大的莊園，沒

- earn (v.) (因自己的努力) 取得；賺
- embark on (v.) 本意為「上船」，現在多用以形容旅程的開始
- involve (v.) 和……有關；牽扯到
- sensor (n.) 感應器
- anti-theft (adj.) 防盜的
- device (n.) 儀器；簡單的機器
- scale (n.) 規模
- security (n.) 保全；安全
- due to (conj.) 由於
- hijack (v.) 劫持 (車輛或飛機)
- contract (n.) 契約；合約；合同

Eventually John earned his Ph.D. and I earned mine, and we embarked on our separate careers. John's research involved sensors; shortly after graduation he started a company that used sensors to make anti-theft devices. Soon he began using computers on a large scale. His business got bigger and bigger until he became head of the largest security system company in America. Due to problems in the Middle East, American planes were hijacked by terrorists several times. John's company won a big contract to design security systems for major American airports. About twenty years after getting his degree, he was worth nearly $400 million.

One year, just before Christmas, I decided to pay John a visit. He happily agreed to host me. First I went to his office, where he gave me a personal tour of his company's showroom. There I discovered that his company made nearly all the car alarm systems on the market. Their tracking device was tiny; if a child took it with him, his parents would always know where he was. I also learned that his company had designed security systems for many American prisons to prevent the inmates from escaping.

Once I had seen the showroom, John drove me to his house. The weather grew stormy, and snowflakes began to fall. John lived in an affluent part of rural New York. When he pointed out his house

6-10

- degree (n.) 學位
- host (v.) 接待
- alarm (n.) 警報器
- track (v.) 追蹤
- tiny (adj.) 很小的
- prison (n.) 監獄
- prevent (v.) 防止（與 from 連用）
- inmate (n.) 囚犯
- snowflake (n.) 雪花
- affluent (adj.) 富裕的

有一點圍牆，可是誰都看出這是私人土地，告示牌也寫得一清二楚，有保全系統，閒人莫入。約翰告訴我他的家有三層紅外線的保護，除非開飛機，否則絕不可能闖入的，如果硬闖的話，不僅附近的警衛會知道，家裡的挪威納犬也會大舉出動，我這才知道約翰的公司會代人訓練這些長像兇猛的狗。

　　約翰的太太在門口迎接我，我們一見如故。他們的家當然是優雅之至，一進門，迎面而來的就是一個明朝的青花瓷花瓶，花瓶裡插滿了長莖的鮮花，後來才發現約翰夫婦愛上了明朝的青花瓷，滿屋子都是，他們的壁紙也一概用淡色的小花為主，彷彿是配這些青花瓷的。

　　我住的客房，附設了一個浴室，這間浴室的洗澡盆和洗臉盆都是仿製青花瓷，約翰告訴我這是他從日本訂作來的，他還訂作了一個青花瓷器，一按，肥皂水就出來了。浴室的瓷磚來自伊朗，也是青色的，

◇ trespass (v.) 不經允許而擅入
◇ layer (n.) 層
◇ infrared (adj.) 紅外線的
◇ laser (n.) 雷射
◇ sneak in (v.) 偷偷進去

◇ intruder (n.) 侵入者
◇ force (n.) 暴力；武力
◇ fierce (v.) 兇猛的
◇ elegant (adj.) 雅緻的；講究的

to me I felt like I was watching a movie. His enormous yard had no wall around it, but anyone could see that it was private property. A sign clearly stated, "Security system—no trespassing." John told me that his house was protected by three layers of infrared lasers—no one could possibly sneak in unless he came on an airplane. And if an intruder entered by force, not only would the neighborhood guard be notified, the Rottweilers in the house would be set loose as well. That was how I learned that John's company trained those fierce-looking dogs for its clients.

John's wife met me at the door, just like old times. It goes without saying that their home was extremely elegant. Inside the door, I was greeted by a blue-flowered porcelain Ming vase filled with fresh long-stemmed flowers. I soon learned that John and his wife had fallen in love with blue-flowered Ming porcelain—it was all over the house. Even their wallpaper was adorned with little pale blossoms, as if to match the porcelain.

My guest room had a private bathroom in which the bathtub and face-washing dish were made to resemble blue-flowered porcelain. John said he had specially ordered them from Japan. He had also ordered a blue-flowered porcelain container: when you pressed it down, liquid soap came out. The bathroom tile came from Iran and

---

◇ long-stemmed (adj.) 長梗的(stem 意　　　◇ dish (n.) 盆
　　為「莖」)　　　　　　　　　　　　　　◇ resemble (v.) 和……類似
◇ adorn (v.) 裝飾；點綴　　　　　　　　　◇ liquid (adj.) 液體
◇ pale (adj.) 蒼白的；淡色的　　　　　　　◇ tile (n.) 瓦；磁磚
◇ blossom (n.) 花

聽說伊朗某一皇宮外牆就用這種瓷磚，我不敢問他們是否這也是訂作的。

這座豪宅當然有極為複雜的安全系統，我發現，入夜以後，最好不要四處走動，恐怕連到廚房裡拿杯水喝都不可能，必須打電話給主人，由他解除了系統，才可以去。

約翰家裡靜得不得了，聽不到任何聲音，可是每隔一小時，他們的落地鐘就會敲出悅耳的聲音，這個鐘聲和倫敦國會大廈的大鵬鐘一模一樣。

11-15　約翰唯一的女兒在哈佛念書，那一天照理說會開車回來，到了六點，還沒有到家，他們夫婦都有點不安。原來這個女孩子厭惡有錢人的生活方式，開一部老爺車，也不肯帶行動電話。他們擔心她老爺車會中途拋錨。

我們一直等到八點，才接到女孩子的電話，果真她的車子壞了，可是她現在安然無恙，在人家家裡，要約翰去接她。約翰弄清楚地址以後，就要我一起去接他女兒，雪已經下得很大了，他女兒落腳的地方是一幢小房子，屋主是個年輕的男孩，一臉年輕人的稚氣表情。

◇ equip (v.) 裝備
◇ shut off (v.) 關掉
◇ chime (n.) 敲鐘的聲音
◇ replica (n.) 複製品

◇ disdain (v.) 不屑
◇ beat-up (adj.) 破舊的
◇ refuse (v.) 拒絕
◇ break down (v.) 拋錨

was also blue. I'd heard that the wall around a certain palace in Iran was adorned with the same kind of tiles. I didn't dare ask if they had specially ordered the tiles too.

Of course, the house was equipped with a highly complex security system. It was best not to walk around at night, I discovered. Even getting a glass of water from the kitchen was impossible—you had to call the owner on the phone and have him shut off the alarm first.

John's house was extremely quiet: no noises could be heard there except for the lovely hourly chimes of their grandfather clock. The clock was a miniature replica of Big Ben by the Houses of Parliament in London.

John's only daughter, a Harvard student, was supposed to drive home that day. At six o'clock, however, she had yet to arrive, and John and his wife were getting worried. Disdaining to live like a rich girl, their daughter drove an old beat-up car and refused to use a cell phone. They worried that her car might have broken down.

It was eight o'clock when we finally got a phone call from her. Sure enough, she had had car trouble, but now she was safe in someone's house. She asked John to come get her. Once he figured out the address, John asked me to go with him to pick up his daughter. The snow was coming down hard now. The place where his daughter had taken refuge was a small house inhabited by a boyish-looking young man.

◇ refuge (n.) 庇護　　　　　　◇ inhabit (v.) 居住

他女兒告訴我們，她車子壞了以後，就去呼救，沒想到家家戶戶都裝了爸爸公司設計的安全系統，使她完全無法可施。總算有一家門口有一個對講機，可是屋主坦白地表示自己是一個弱女子，在等她丈夫回來，不敢讓她進門，因為她不知道會不會受騙。

他女兒說當她被拒的時候，她相信家家戶戶都在放聖誕音樂——平安夜，聖善夜——聖誕節應該是充滿了愛與關懷的日子，可是她卻被大家拒於千里之外，虧得她最後找到了這一座又破又舊的小房子，她知道這座小房子是不會用安全系統的，果然也遇見了這位和氣而友善的屋主。

這位年輕的男孩子一面給我熱茶喝，一面發表他一個奇特的看法，他說家家戶戶都裝了安全系統，耶穌會到那裡去降生呢？可憐的聖母瑪利亞，可能連馬槽都找不到。

16-20　約翰聽了這些話，當然很不是滋味，可是他一再謝謝這位好心的年輕人，也邀他一起去吃晚飯，年輕人一聽到有人請他吃晚飯，立刻答

◇ intercom (n.) 對講機
◇ frankly (adv.) 坦白地；誠然地
◇ vulnerable (adj.) 容易被欺負、攻擊或傷害的
◇ trick (n.) 詭計
◇ turn away (v.) 拒絕
◇ shabby (adj.) 破舊的
◇ cottage (n.) 小房子

John's daughter told us that when her car broke down, she had gone to look for help. But she couldn't find anyone to help her—the houses in the area were all protected by security systems from her father's company. At last she found a house with an intercom by the front door, but its owner told her frankly that she was a vulnerable woman waiting for her husband to come home, and she didn't dare let her in because it might be a trick.

John's daughter said that when she was turned away, she thought of how everyone was probably listening to Christmas songs at home— "Silent night, holy night" and all. Christmas was supposed to be a day of love and caring, but she had been completely shut out. Fortunately, she finally found a shabby old cottage that she knew would not have a security system. And she was right—she had found this kind, affable young man.

As he poured me some hot tea, this young man expressed a peculiar thought. If every house had a security system, he said, where would Jesus go to be born? Poor Saint Mary might not even be able to find a stable.

John, of course, was none too pleased by this remark. Nevertheless, he heartily thanked the young man for his kindness and invited him over for dinner. The young man jumped at the chance for a free meal.

16-20

- affable (adj.) 友善的
- peculiar (adj.) 奇特的
- stable (n.) 馬廄
- remark (n.) 評論
- heartily (adv.) 熱情地

應了，我想起我年輕的時候，也是如此，從未拒絕過任何一頓晚飯的邀約。

晚餐在一張長桌上吃的，夫妻兩人分坐長桌的兩端，一位臉上沒有表情穿制服的僕人來回送菜，每一道菜都是精點，每一種餐具更是講究無比，可是我想起當年我們在約翰家廚房吃晚飯情形，我覺得當年的飯好吃多了。

約翰的女兒顯得有點不自然，那位年輕人卻是最快樂的人，有多少吃多少，一副不吃白不吃的表情，吃完飯，已經十點了，約翰的女兒將年輕人送回家。我卻有一個疑問，那些可愛的瓷娃娃到那裡去了？我不敢問，因為答案一定是很尷尬的。

第二天約翰送我到機場，他似乎稍微沉默了一點。下了汽車，他撞到另一部汽車，立刻警鈴大作，這又是他的傑作，自作自受地。我假裝沒有聽到，可是我看到他一臉不自然的表情。

他也無法送我去候機室，安全系統規定送客者早就該留步了。

◇ dish (n.) 菜餚
◇ tableware (n.) 餐具
◇ ill at ease (adj.) 不自在
◇ pass up (v.) 錯過

◇ linger (v.) 徘徊
◇ adorable (adj.) 可愛的
◇ awkward (adj.) 尷尬的

I was reminded of my own youth, when I was the same way—I never turned down an invitation for dinner.

Dinner was served at a long table. John and his wife sat at the ends, and a uniformed servant served the food with a blank expression. Each dish was a work of art, as was each piece of tableware. Yet when I thought of the meals I had eaten in John's kitchen years ago, I felt like the food had tasted much better then.

John's daughter appeared rather ill at ease, but the young man was the happiest person at the table. "Why pass up any of this delicious food?" his face seemed to say. It was ten o'clock by the time we finished. John's daughter drove the young man home. A question lingered in my mind: what had happened to those adorable porcelain dolls? I didn't dare to ask because the answer was no doubt an awkward one.

The next day, as John drove me to the airport, he seemed a little quieter. When he got out of the car, he bumped into another car, whose alarm promptly went off. Here was yet another of his masterpieces—and he had only himself to blame. I pretended not to hear, but I saw the look of chagrin on his face.

He couldn't accompany me to the departure lounge—the airport security system prevented him from escorting me that far.

◇ bump (v.) 輕輕地撞
◇ promptly (adv.) 立即地；很快地
◇ blame (v.) 責怪
◇ chagrin (n.) 糗
◇ accompany (v.) 陪
◇ escort (v.) 護送；陪同

21-25　　一年以後，我忽然在《華爾街日報》上看到一則消息，約翰將他的公司賣掉了，他一夜間得到了四億多美金，他的豪華住宅賣了五百萬美金，約翰在記者會上宣布，他留下一個零頭，用四億多美金成立一個慈善基金會，基金會的董事們全是社會上有頭有臉的人，他不是董事，他也不會過問這個基金會如何行善，他完全信任這些董事們。

　　幾天以後，約翰夫婦就消失了，他的親人替他們保密行蹤，他的女兒已和那位年輕人結了婚，到非洲去幫助窮人了，這位科技名人就此失蹤了。

　　可是我有把握約翰會找我的，因為我們的友誼比較特別，果真我收到他的信了，他告訴我他現在住在英國一個偏遠的鄉下，這裡沒有一家人用安全系統，他給我他的電話和地址，可是他故意不給我他的門牌號碼，他叫我去拜訪他們夫婦二人，而且他說我一定會找到他家的。

◇ out of the blue (adv.) 忽然
◇ mansion (n.) 豪宅
◇ press conference (n.) 記者會
◇ announce (v.) 宣布
◇ charitable (adj.) 慈善的

◇ foundation (n.) 基金會
◇ board of directors (n.) 董事會 (簡稱 board)
◇ outstanding (adj.) 出色的；優秀的

A year later, out of the blue, I read in *The Wall Street Journal* that John had sold his company for more than $400 million. His mansion sold for $5 million. At a press conference, John announced that he planned to keep a small amount of money for himself and use the rest of the $400 million to establish a charitable foundation. The foundation would be run by a board of directors comprised of various outstanding members of society. He was not a member of the board, and he was not going to overly concern himself with what sort of philanthropy the charity involved itself in. The board had his full trust.

A few days later, John and his wife disappeared. Their family kept their whereabouts a secret. John's daughter married the young man and moved to Africa to help the poor. Just like that, a technological celebrity was gone without a trace.

But I knew that John would want to see me again because our friendship was special. Sure enough, I received a letter from him. He wrote that he was now living in a secluded English village where nobody had a security system. He gave me his phone number and address, but he intentionally omitted his house number. He asked me to come visit him and his wife, assuring me that I would be able to find their house.

◇ philanthropy (n.) 造福人群的工作　　◇ omit (v.) 遺漏
◇ trace (n.) 痕跡　　◇ assure (v.) (以說話) 使 (人家) 放心
◇ secluded (adj.) 僻靜的
◇ intentionally (adv.) 故意地

　　我找了一個機會去英國開會，也和約翰約好了去看他的時間。下了火車，我找到了那條街，那條街的一邊面對一大片山谷，沒有一幢房子，所以我只要看街的另一邊就可以了。

　　我在街上閒逛，忽然看到一幢房子的落地大玻璃窗與眾不同，因為這個窗檯上放滿了瓷娃娃，好可愛的瓷娃娃，我想這一定是一家舊貨店，我想起約翰夫婦喜歡瓷娃娃，決定進去買一個送他們。沒有想到當我抬起頭來的時候，我看到約翰在裡面，這不是舊貨店，這是他們的家，只是他們的家完全對外開放，又放滿了瓷娃娃，才使我誤解了。

26-30　　約翰夫婦熱情地招待我，他們的家比以前的豪宅小太多了，據他們說，這座小房子比他們當年佣人住的房子還小，也比他們當年的花房小，我記起他們家在冬天也有如此多的花，原來是有花房的緣故。

　　他們的明朝青花瓷器完全不見了，約翰夫婦將那些瓷器捐給了紐約的一家博物館，他們夫婦二人認為人類文明的結晶，應該由人類全體所共享。

◇ stroll (v.) 散步
◇ stand out (v.) 引人注目
◇ astonishment (n.) 驚訝
◇ mislead (v.) 誤導；騙

I looked for an opportunity to attend a meeting in England, and I arranged a meeting time with John. I stepped off the train and found the street he lived on. One side of the street faced a large valley and thus had no houses; all I had to do was look at the houses on the other side.

As I strolled down the street, I suddenly noticed a house with a large French window in front. It stood out because of all the cute porcelain dolls standing on its windowsill. I figured it must be a secondhand shop, and I decided to buy a doll there for John. To my astonishment, when I lifted my head to look in, I saw John inside! It wasn't a secondhand shop at all—it was his house. The dolls and the openness of the house had misled me into thinking it was a shop.

John and his wife received me enthusiastically. Their new house was tiny compared to their old one. They said it was smaller than the house where their servants had lived, smaller even than their greenhouse. I recalled how even in winter their old house had been filled with flowers—evidently they came from the greenhouse.

26-30

Their blue-flowered Ming porcelains were all gone: John and his wife had donated them to a museum in New York. It was their opinion that the treasures of human civilization should be enjoyed by humankind as a whole.

◇ enthusiastically (adv.) 熱情地
◇ greenhouse (n.) 花房；溫室
◇ donate (v.) 捐
◇ treasure (n.) 寶藏

他們的園子也小得很，可是約翰夫婦仍然在園子裡種了花草，他們的後園對著一大片森林，約翰說據說當年羅賓漢就出沒在這一片森林裡，而他們所面對的山谷由英國詩人協會所擁有，他們不會開發這片荒原的，因為英國人喜歡荒原，約翰夫婦也養成了在荒原中散步的習慣。

約翰告訴我為什麼他最後決定放棄一切。他的公司得到了一個大合同，改善整個加州監獄的安全系統，他發現了加州花在監獄上的錢比花在教育上的還多。而他呢？他越來越有錢，卻越來越像住在一座監獄裡面。美國人一向標榜「自由而且開放」的社會，其實美國人卻越來越將自己封閉起來，越來越使自己失去自由。約翰決心不再拼命賺錢，只為了找回失去了好久的自由。

約翰夫婦在附近的一家高中教書，這所學校其實有點像專科學校，約翰教線路設計，學生所設計出來的線路經常得獎，他捐了很多錢給這所學校，使這所學校有很好的圖書館和實驗室，他太太在那裡教英文。

◇ supposedly（adv.）據說
◇ very（adj.）正是
◇ tract（n.）大片（土地）
◇ moorland（n.）（英國特有的）荒野（也可寫作 moor）
◇ boast of（v.）標榜
◇ seal up（v.）封閉起來
◇ devote（v.）奉獻
◇ reclaim（v.）取回
◇ circuit（n.）線路

Their yard was small too, but they had planted it with grass and flowers anyway. Their backyard faced a huge forest—John said it was supposedly the very forest that Robin Hood had once called home. The valley across the road was owned by the English Poetry Society. They would not develop this tract of moorland because the English are fond of moors. John and his wife had developed a habit of taking walks over the moor.

John told me why he had finally decided to give it all up. When his company won a big contract to improve security systems for the entire California prison system, he found out that California spends more money on prisons than on education. Meanwhile, he grew richer and richer, but felt more and more like he lived in a prison himself. Americans had always boasted of their "free and open" society, but in reality Americans were sealing themselves up more and more, gradually taking away their own freedom. John decided to stop devoting so much effort to making money—all he wanted was to reclaim the freedom he had lost for so long.

John and his wife were teachers at a high school—actually, it was more like a technical school—in their neighborhood. John taught circuit design, and the circuits his students designed frequently won prizes. He donated a good deal of money to the school to ensure that its library and laboratories would be first-rate. His wife was an English teacher.

◇ ensure (v.) 確保
◇ laboratory (n.) 實驗室
◇ first-rate (adj.) 一流的

31-35　　約翰告訴我他們兩人的薪水就足足應付他們的生活了，因為他們生活得很簡單，平時騎自行車上班，連汽油都用得很少。

　　當我們坐下來吃晚飯的時候，我才發現我的那座女孩子瓷娃娃放在桌子中間。他們當時念舊，捨不得丟掉那些瓷娃娃，可是替他們設計內部裝潢的設計師不讓他擺設這些不值錢的東西。現在那些值錢的東西都不見了，不值錢的瓷娃娃又出現了。

　　我總算吃到了我當年常吃到的晚飯，也重新享受到約翰夫婦家中的溫暖。

　　我離開的時候，約翰送我去火車站，他告訴我他還有一些錢，他的女兒不會要他的這些錢，等他和太太都去世了，他的錢就全部捐出去了。

　　我說我好佩服他，因為他已經捐出他的全部所有，他忽然一笑，告訴我他仍然有一樣寶物，沒有捐掉。我對此大為好奇，問他是什麼，他說他要賣一個關子，他用一張小紙寫了下來，交給我，但叫我現在不要看，等火車開了以後再看，上面寫的是他不會捐出去的寶物。

◇ combined (adj.) 合起來的　　　　◇ display (v.) 陳列；擺出
◇ part (v.) 分開　　　　　　　　　◇ trinket (n.) 不值錢的玩意

John told me that he and his wife's combined income was more   31-35
than enough to meet their needs because they lived simply. Usually
they bicycled to work; they rarely used their car.

When we sat down to have dinner together, I saw that they had
placed my maiden doll in the center of their table. They had been
unwilling to part with their porcelain dolls while in school, but the
designer who planned the interior of their mansion refused to let them
display such cheap trinkets. Now the valuable decorations were all
gone, and the cheap porcelain dolls had reappeared.

I finally got to eat a meal like John's wife used to fix in the first
years of our friendship, and I enjoyed the warmth of their home once
more.

When I left, John drove me to the train station. He told me that he
still had some money, but his daughter wasn't going to want it. When
he and his wife died, all the money he had left would be donated.

I told him I admired him for donating all that he had. Suddenly
he laughed, and he told me he had kept one treasure for himself. My
curiosity aroused, I asked him what it was. He said that he wanted to
keep me in suspense for a while. He wrote something on a piece of
paper and gave the paper to me, but he said I couldn't read it until the
train left. On it was written the treasure he had kept for himself.

◇ reappear (v.) 再次出現   ◇ suspense (n.) 懸疑
◇ arouse (v.) 激起

36-37　　火車開了，我和站在月台上的約翰揮手再見，等我看不見他以後，打開了那張紙，紙上寫的是「我的靈魂」。

　　我坐在火車裡，不禁一直想著，有些人什麼都有，卻失落了自己的靈魂。

◇ reflect (v.) 思考，反省

The train pulled away; I waved goodbye to John on the platform. Once he was out of sight, I opened the paper. On it was written, "My soul."

As I sat inside the train, I couldn't help reflecting: some people have everything, but they've forgotten all about their souls.

（1） the two of them 他們兩人（1 段）

The two of them often invited me over for meals.

他們常邀我到他家吃飯。

解析

在中文，數詞在代名詞之後，例如：「我們兩個；他們四個。」但在英文中，數詞通常在前，後面接 of，清楚表示出數量。

◇ 我們這個週末要去旅行，所以你們四個必須看家。
　 We're going on a trip this weekend, so the four of you will have to take care of the house.

如何用英文表達約翰夫婦呢？當然不能直譯為 John husband and wife 或是 Mr. and Mrs. John。這裡寫成 John and his wife，或直接說 the two of them 都可清楚的表達。

小試身手

1-1. 這個學期我們三個都上一樣的課。

_____

1-2. 她嫁給他先生的隔天，兩人就去度蜜月。

_____

（2） have a tendency to... 有⋯⋯的傾向（3 段）

Lladró's famous figurines had a tendency to be tall, thin and melancholy-looking.

這家名牌公司的娃娃個個又高又瘦，也都帶憂鬱的表情。

解析

tendency（傾向）的動詞形式是 tend。那為何不直接用 tended 就好，而要用 had a tendency？其實，你可以這樣用，句子還是對的：

Lladró's famous figurines tended to be tall, thin and melancholy-looking.

兩種形式都很常見，也可互換。怎麼決定用哪一個？基本上，那只是一種習慣與各人喜好罷了。那為何不把原文提到的「個個」翻成 every one of...？嗯，我認為這樣就有點太過強調了。用 tendency 這個字來軟化這個描述，聽起來比較合理。這裡有另一個例子，如果某人常常感到憂煩，你可跟他(她)說：

◇ 你總是太過操心了。
　 You have a tendency to worry too much.

與其說 Stop worrying all the time.（不要老是煩惱），上個句子聽起來好聽多啦。

另一件值得注意的，是複合形容詞 "melancholy-looking"。在前幾篇裡，我曾解釋如何用連字號（hyphen）連結兩個字來創造一個形容詞。我用 melancholy-looking 來表達「帶著憂鬱的表情」，而不會妨礙句子的流暢度。要不然，這句子會非常冗長：

Lladró's famous figurines tended to be tall and thin and wear melancholy expressions on their faces.

即然有簡潔的用法，為什麼要在同一個段落重覆兩次一樣的描述？

小試身手

2-1. 有錢的外國商人大部分都很胖。

_____

2-2. 她是個看起來很聰明的小孩。

_____

（3）pay a visit 拜訪（5 段）

One year, just before Christmas, I decided to pay John a visit.

有一年，我決定去找他……那時已近耶誕節。

解析

這個用法很有意思——讓我想到中文的「拜訪，拜年」，都顯現出對出訪朋友的敬意。pay 這個字讓我們覺得敘事者身為一個這麼要好的朋友，彷彿「欠」了 John 的恩情似的，非得去拜訪他來還這個人情債。但記住，**pay a visit** 是慣用語，也可用於一般的拜訪。

小試身手

3. 今天我要去拜訪一位老朋友。

_____

（4）sneak 偷偷移動

No one could possibly sneak in unless he came on an airplane.

除非乘飛機，否則絕不可能闖入的。

解析

你可以把 sneak 當成 walk 或 move，只不過 sneak 是「鬼鬼祟祟地移動」。然而跟那些動詞不同的是，sneak 一定會接介系詞。以下例子可以清楚說明這點：

◇ 她喜歡闖入空盪的屋子裡遊蕩。
　 She likes to sneak around empty houses.

◇ 他想逃學的時候被逮個正著。
　 He got caught trying to sneak out of school.

◇ 不要那樣鬼鬼祟祟地看我！
　 Don't sneak up on me like that!

如果沒介詞的話，你就無法知道哪裡或為何主詞要 sneak，而我們總是要有 sneak 的原因啊！此要，注意 sneak 是不規則動詞，過去式是 snuck。

小試身手

4-1. 你有沒有沒付錢偷溜進電影院過？

_____

4-2. 你為什麼在晚上鬼鬼祟祟地走來走去？

_____

（5）it goes without saying that... 當然……（7 段）

It goes without saying that their home was extremely elegant.

他們的家當然是優雅之至。

解析

哪一種房子得花4億才能住得起？當然是莊園，裡頭有漂亮的家具、藝術品和各色舒服的設備。敘事者知道我們了解，所以在句中他用「當然」一詞。如果我直譯，那可翻成 of course 或 naturally，但在此我認為用 it goes without saying 來表示「不用我說你就知道」更好。這片語用在很明顯但又不得不說的狀況。以下是另一個例子：

◇ 喝醉的司機當然比清醒的司機更危險。
It goes without saying that drunk drivers are more dangerous than sober ones.

另一個相關片語 needless to say 也表示同樣意思。

◇ 我不小心打破了她最愛的花瓶。她當然很不高興。
I accidentally broke her favorite vase. Needless to say, she was upset.

小試身手

5. 不消說，他對中國政府提出的批評使他在中國不甚受歡迎。

_____

（6）supposed to... 應該……（11 段；14 段）

John's only daughter, a Harvard student, was supposed to drive home that day.
約翰唯一的女兒在哈佛念書，那一天照理說會開車回來。

Christmas was supposed to be a day of love and caring, but she had been completely shut out.
聖誕節應該是充滿了愛與關懷的日子，可是她卻被大家拒於千里之外。

解析

概括來說，「應該是」表示某事是被預期朝某方向發展的。有時候，特別是談論某人時，「應該是」更帶著有此義務的弦外之音。如果聽起來有點含糊，上面第一句指的是人——約翰的女兒。大家預期她那天該開車回來，當她沒出現時，父母親自然假設她出事了。第二句指的是事情——耶誕節。每個人都預設耶誕節是個充滿愛與關懷的節日，因為這是傳統。然而，當約翰的女兒困在雪中，無人救援時，她當然會覺得耶誕節不應該是這樣的，很像耶誕節故意「為難」她似的。

以下例子可進一步說明我的意思。

◇ 你不應該未經准許而開這輛車。
　　You're not supposed to drive the car without permission.

◇ 根據天氣預報，明天應該會下雨。
　　According to the weather forecast, it's supposed to rain tomorrow.

小試身手

6-1. 童話應該有「快樂到永遠」的結局才對。

　　_____

6-2. 遇到節日你就要休息，不要加班。

　　_____

6-3. 電腦的功能不正常。

　　_____

6-4. 他今天下午本來應該要打電話給我。

　　_____

---

(7) none too... 不太；一點也不(16 段)

John, of course, was none too pleased by this remark.

約翰聽了這些話，當然很不是滋味。

解析

這裡不用 not very 或簡單的 not，而用 none too 這個比較有意思的用法。我們只知道約翰不高興，有多不高興，任君想像。當我們用這個片語時，後面記得要加形容詞。

◇ 當我的父母發現我輟學時，他們一點也不高興。
My parents were none too happy when they found out I had quit school.

小試身手

7. 他是個很好的男孩子，只是不太聰明。

_____

(8) yet another 又一個(19 段)

Here was yet another of his masterpieces—and he had only himself to blame.

這又是他的傑作，自作自受地。

解析

以下三句可以清楚說明 yet another 的用法：First he made a mistake.（他犯錯。）Then he made another mistake.（他再犯了錯。）Then he made yet another mistake.（他又犯了錯。）

如同我們這裡看到的，yet another 更強調「另一個」。而犯下 yet another mistake 之前，他得至少先犯兩個錯。

◇ 空氣污染又是另一個我不喜歡住城市的理由。（意味另有其他原因）
Air pollution is yet another reason why I don't like living in the city.

◇ 瑪莉姑姑又買了一個錢包？她到底有幾個錢包？
Aunt Mary bought yet another purse? How many purses does she have?

小試身手

8. 我簡直無法相信他們又要去夏威夷旅行！

_____

(9) 動詞 + 反身代名詞(21 段)

He was not a member of the board, and he was not going to overly concern himself with what sort of philanthropy the charity involved itself in.

他不是董事,他也不會過問這個基金會如何行善。

解析

這個長句乍看很複雜,其實並不會。只要知道 concern 和 involve 後面接反身代名詞就行了。如同你知道的,concern 是「擔心、關心」的意思,另外一個意思是「和……有關係」:

◇ 我擔心你身體的狀況。
　 I'm concerned about your health.

◇ 這個對話和你沒有關係。
　 This conversation doesn't concern you.

現在如果我們在 concern 之後加上反身代名詞 himself,會怎樣呢?從故事裡的句子來說,約翰說對於他的基金會的作為,他將不至於 overly concern himself。這表示他不會太過擔心,也不會干涉其中運作。

中文裡所謂「愛管閒事」可以把它翻成很長的句子: "He tends to concern himself with things that are none of his business." 基本上,不讓你自己擔心太多事是好的——要不然你所有的憂慮只會增添你的壓力。總結來說,to concern oneself with something 就是決定去操心或去涉入了。

讀了以上幾段,你現在應該可以自己找出 involve oneself 的意思了吧!只要你知道 involve 是「和……有關係」的意思,你就知道 itself 指的是故事中的基金會。

小試身手

9-1. 你不應該去管你老闆的私人生活。

_____

9-2. 她給自己提名 (nominate) 當會長。

_____

9-3. 我常常自我承擔別人的問題。

_____

(10) more than enough 不但足夠而且有餘 (31 段)

John told me that he and his wife's combined income was more than enough to meet their needs because they lived simply.

約翰告訴我他們兩人的薪水就足足應付他們的生活了，因為他們生活得很簡單。

解析

這個簡單的片語值得一提，如果沒有 more than 兩字，這句話聽起來就像約翰和妻子兩人賺的錢僅供溫飽而已。但 more than enough 給人餘裕之感。請見另一例：

◇ 別擔心，我的時間很多，跟你練習英文絕對沒問題。
　　Don't worry, I have more than enough time to practice English with you.

小試身手

10. 歡迎你和我們家一起吃飯。媽媽總會煮很多，全家吃飽了還會有剩。

_____

(11) keep sb in suspense 賣關子(35 段)

He said that he wanted to keep me in suspense for a while.
他說他要賣個關子。

解析

哎呀，在沒有說書傳統的美國，「賣個關子」要怎麼翻譯？簡單，你只需要 suspense(懸疑)這個字。作者喜歡在每章結尾賣個關子，好吸引讀者讀下去。而在這故事裡，約翰不只賣朋友關子，也讓所有讀者不明究裡──我們得繼續看下去才知道有啥寶物約翰沒有捐出去。再次強調，這個片語簡單卻很有用喔。

小試身手

11. 我愛她的偵探小說，因為它們充滿了永無止境的懸疑。

_____

(12) out of sight 不見蹤影(36 段)

Once he was out of sight, I opened the paper.
等我看不見他以後，打開了那張紙。

解析

英文有個諺語 "Out of sight, out of mind." 意思是你沒看到的東西，常就會容易被遺忘。sight 當然指的是「視力能夠到達的範圍」，你看得到的東西都算 in sight；當你不再看到某個東西，就是 out of sight。另一個類似指「聽不到」的片語則是 out of earshot。

小試身手

12-1. 不要說她的八卦，除非你確定她聽不見。

_____

12-2. 這裡真是沙漠，一株植物也看不見。

_____

 小試身手解答

1-1. The three of us are taking the same classes this semester.

1-2. The day after she married her husband, the two of them set off on their honeymoon.

2-1. Foreign businessmen tend to be overweight.

2-2. She is an intelligent-looking girl.

3. Today I'm going to pay a visit to an old friend.

4-1. Have you ever snuck into a movie without paying?

4-2. Why are you sneaking around in the dark?

5. Needless to say, his criticisms of China government made him unpopular in China.

6-1. Fairy tales are supposed to end with "happily ever after."

6-2. You're supposed to rest on holidays, not work overtime.

6-3. The computer isn't working like it's supposed to.

6-4. He was supposed to call me this afternoon.

7. He's a nice boy, but he's none too bright.

8. I can't believe they're going on yet another vacation to Hawaii!

9-1. You shouldn't concern yourself with your boss's personal life.

9-2.　She nominated herself for president.

9-3.　I tend to burden myself with other people's problems.

10.　　You're welcome to have dinner with us—Mom always cooks more than enough to feed our family.

11.　　I love her detective novels because they keep me in perpetual suspense.

12-1. Don't gossip about her unless you're sure she's out of earshot.

12-2. This sure is a desert—there isn't a plant in sight.

I'm Me
我是我

1-5　　　回想起來，我的童年應該是比同年紀的德國孩子要舒服得多。我是德國人，五歲的時候，正值二次大戰，爸爸在蘇聯境內陣亡了，六歲的時候，我唯一的哥哥也陣亡了，我和我的母親相依為命。在二次大戰期間，這不是什麼了不起的事，我的鄰居玩伴們，幾乎都失去了爸爸，即使爸爸或大哥哥還活著，也都是在前線打仗。

　　我還記得在我八歲的時候，日子越來越不好過，本來店裡可以買到很多東西，現在東西越來越少。我記得有一次媽媽帶我去一家百貨公司，裡面幾乎都是空的，連玩具都少得不得了。

　　可是我們家似乎一直受到政府的特別照顧，每三天，就有人送食物來，鄰居都羨慕我們，他們很難買到牛奶和肉，我和我母親卻從來不缺乏牛奶和肉，我甚至一直吃到巧克力糖，我知道鄰居早已吃不到蛋糕了，我們卻過一陣子就有人送蛋糕來，據我記憶所知，媽媽從不需要上街買菜。

　　我六歲進小學，念的是柏林城裡最好的小學，每天早上，有一個小兵開車送我去，放學時也有小兵接我回來。我雖然小，也知道我們的

CD2-6

◇ pleasant (adj.)愉快的(動詞為please)
◇ action (n.)這裡指戰鬥；killed in action是代表「陣亡」的慣用語
◇ stock (v.) 進貨；存貨
◇ goods (n.) 貨品 (常用複數)
◇ next to nothing (adv.) 幾乎沒有

Looking back, I must have had a pleasanter childhood than most German children my age. I'm a German; when I was five, during World War II, my father was killed in action; when I was six, my only brother died the same way. My mother and I did our best to take care of each other. Our situation was hardly unusual—nearly all my neighborhood friends had lost their fathers in the war too. Even if their fathers or older brothers were still alive, they were fighting on the front lines.

I remember that life became especially difficult the year I turned eight. Stores that were once well stocked with goods grew emptier and emptier. I'll always remember the time when Mother took me to a department store and there was next to nothing inside—even the toys were almost gone.

But it always seemed like the government took especially good care of our family. Food was brought to us every three days. Our neighbors envied us—they had a devil of a time trying to buy milk and meat, but my mother and I never ran short of either. I could even get chocolates when I wanted them. Every so often, a cake would be delivered to us; our neighbors hadn't been able to eat cake for years. I can't remember a single time when Mother had to shop for us.

At six I started school, the best elementary school in Berlin. Each morning, a soldier would drive me to school, and when class ended a soldier would come and drive me home. Though I was only a child,

◇ envy (v.) 羨慕；忌妒　　　　　　◇ deliver (v.) 運送
◇ run short of (v.) 缺乏 (常用的東西)

情況非常特殊，我問我母親為什麼政府如此的照顧我們，他說：「傻小子，難道你不知道你爸爸和哥哥都替國家犧牲了性命？政府當然會對我們好的。」我可不太相信媽媽的話，理由很簡單，我的同學也失去了爸爸和哥哥，他們為什麼沒有人送食物來？也沒有小兵開車送他們上學。

到後來砲聲越來越清晰。媽媽偷偷告訴我，俄國軍已經逼近。有一天，媽媽告訴我，柏林城所有的學校都已經關閉，事實上我上課的小學只有一半教室可以用。我記得最後一次上課，正好碰到空襲，我們在地下室躲了兩個小時，出來的時候，發現附近到處大火，我們都無心上課，只等家人來接我們回去。

6-10　　砲聲聽起來越來越近，媽媽也越來越焦慮。我當時還是小孩，還不懂什麼是害怕，看到外面軍隊調動，還有些興奮，可是連我這個小孩子都看得出來，我們德國軍隊是輸定了。看到軍人疲憊不堪的表情，我也很難過。

◇ skeptical (adj.) 有懷疑的
◇ explanation (n.) 解釋
◇ furtively (adv.) 偷偷地
◇ inform (v.) 告知

◇ draw near (v.) 慢慢靠近
◇ at any rate 無論如何；至少
◇ air raid (n.) 空襲
◇ emerge (v.) (躲完了以後)出來

I knew our family was getting special treatment. I asked Mother why the government took such good care of us, and she said, "Silly boy, don't you know that your father and brother sacrificed their lives for the country? Of course the government treats us well." But I remained skeptical of my mother's explanation. After all, other kids at school had lost their fathers and brothers too—why didn't anyone deliver food to them? Why were there no soldiers to take them to school?

Slowly but surely, the distant sounds of war grew clearer. Mother furtively informed me that the Russian army was drawing near. One day she told me that all the schools in Berlin had been closed. At any rate my school only had half a classroom that could still be used. I still remember how my last class was interrupted by an air raid. For two hours we hid underground. When we emerged, fires were raging all around. No one wanted to continue the class after that—we just waited for our families to come and take us home.

The shelling came nearer, and Mother grew more anxious by the day. I was still too much of a child to understand fear—I actually felt rather excited watching the troops maneuver outside—but even a child could see that Germany was going to lose the war. It made me very sad to see the exhausted looks on the soldiers' faces.

6-10

◇ rage（v.）發怒（名詞 rage 是「怒氣」的意思）
◇ shell（v.）砲擊（聲）
◇ anxious（adj.）焦慮的
◇ maneuver（v.）調動

有一天下午，媽媽忽然告訴我，街上出奇地安靜，一個軍人都看不見，本來我們家門口附近永遠有一個兵在站崗，現在也不見了。更奇怪的是，砲聲也停了，我問媽媽為什麼砲聲停住了，媽媽告訴我大概俄國軍隊馬上就要進城了。

當天晚上，我睡得很熟，因為外面靜到極點，大概早上五點，媽媽把我叫醒，他替我穿好衣服，然後叫我做一件我當時覺得很不可思議的事，他叫我趕快逃離柏林，越快越好。媽媽告訴我該沿一條大路向北走，最好快跑，媽媽說，如果我快步走，大約兩個小時，就可以逃到鄉下，到了鄉下，我應該設法讓一個家庭收容我，媽媽一再強調我必須忘掉爸爸媽媽，不要再回來。當時外面一片漆黑，我當然不肯，大哭起來，可是媽媽最後還是說服了我，他準備了一瓶熱牛奶和兩塊麵包，他說我應該將食物吃掉以後，將熱水瓶丟掉，一定要裝得很可憐的樣子。他送我一個十字架的項鍊掛在脖子上，同時，又塞了一張紙在我的衣服口袋裡。

媽媽和我緊緊擁抱以後，還是趕我走。我走到街上，回頭看媽媽，

◇ eerily (adv.) 詭異地；出奇地
◇ formerly (adv.) 從前
◇ stand guard (v.) 站崗；守衛
◇ fire (v.) 開（槍、砲等）（這裡的firing是名詞，指的是砲聲）
◇ Soviet (n.) 蘇聯人（the Soviet Union 蘇聯）
◇ still (adj.) 寂靜的
◇ utterly (adv.) 徹底地
◇ incredible (adj.) 難以置信的
◇ flee (v.) 逃離
◇ thoroughfare (n.) 大道
◇ stress (v.) 強調

One afternoon, Mother suddenly informed me that the streets had grown eerily quiet—no soldiers could be seen anywhere. Formerly, there had always been a soldier standing guard by our door, but now even he was gone. Stranger still, the firing had stopped. When I asked Mother why, she said it was probably because the Soviets were about to enter the city.

I slept deeply that night, for the night was perfectly still. At about five in the morning, Mother woke me up, put some clothes on me, and told me to do something utterly incredible: flee Berlin immediately, the sooner the better. Mother said I should head north along a main thoroughfare, as fast as my legs could carry me. If I was fast enough, she said, I'd make it to the countryside in about two hours. Once I got there, I was to find a family who would take me in. Mother stressed repeatedly that I should forget her and Father and never come back. It was pitch dark outside—of course I didn't want to go. I started to cry hard, but at last Mother managed to persuade me. She fixed me a bottle of warm milk and two slices of bread and said that when I finished eating I should throw my thermos away and try to look pitiful. She also fastened a crucifix around my neck and stuffed a paper into my pocket.

Mother hugged me tightly, then sent me away. I looked back at her from the street and saw her wiping away tears. But she quickly closed

◇ repeatedly (adv.) 重複地；一再地
◇ pitch dark (adj.) 漆黑的
◇ fix (v.) 準備（飲食）
◇ thermos (n.) 熱水瓶（有的人會將t大寫，因為Thermos是個品牌）
◇ fasten (v.) 繫
◇ crucifix (n.) 十字架（通常有耶穌的雕像掛在上面）
◇ wipe (v.) 擦

發現她正在擦眼淚，可是她很快的關上了門，我知道非走不可了。我念的學校很注重體能訓練，所以我可以快步走很長的路，大約天亮的時候，我聽到砲聲再度大作，可是大概一個小時以後，砲聲忽然全部都停了，我知道俄國軍隊一定進城了，我可以想像得到俄國坦克進城的景象，我當然最擔心的是我的媽媽。

　　鄉下總算到了，我已經累得再也走不動了，我找了一家農舍，發現馬槽大門開著，那時天才亮，鄉下人還沒有出來，我就進入了馬槽，馬槽裡面有一匹馬和一頭牛，牠們對我這個小孩子的入侵者根本不在意，我看上了馬槽裡的一堆稻草，倒上去就睡著了。

11-15　　醒來以後，我發現我躺在一張舒適的床上，一位老太太大概一直坐在我身旁。看見我醒來，向窗外大聲地叫她的丈夫回來，這對慈祥的老夫婦問我是怎麼一回事，我說我父親哥哥都去世，俄國軍隊快進城了，媽媽帶我逃離，因為難民人數相當多，我和媽媽失去了聯絡，媽媽曾告訴我，萬一走散了，應該盡量到鄉下去，那裡總會有好心的農人會收容我的，所以我就往鄉下走來。

◇ be big on (v.) (俚) 重視
◇ dawn (n.) 黎明
◇ boom (n.) 隆隆聲 (狀聲詞)
◇ artillery (n.) 大砲
◇ penetrate (v.) 穿入

◇ stable (n.) 馬廄
◇ inhabitant (n.) 棲居的動物
◇ invasion (n.) 侵入
◇ privacy (n.) 隱私權；隱私空間
◇ pick out (v.) (非正式) 挑選出

the door, and I knew I had to go. My school had been big on physical education, so I had no problem walking fast for a long distance. Around dawn, I heard the boom of artillery once more. After about an hour, however, it suddenly stopped. I knew that meant the Russian army had penetrated the city. In my mind's eye, I could see their tanks rolling in. More than anything, I worried about my mother.

When I finally reached the countryside, I was too exhausted to walk any further. I found a farm where the stable door was open. Dawn had just broken, and the farmers had not yet emerged. I entered the stable, whose inhabitants, a horse and a cow, seemed not to mind my invasion of their privacy. I picked out a nice pile of straw and was out cold in no time.

When I awoke, I found myself lying in a comfortable bed, flanked by an elderly woman who must have kept watch by my side as I slept. Seeing me awaken, she turned toward the window and shouted at her husband to come over. The kind old couple asked me where I had come from. I told them that my father and brother were dead, and my mother had fled Berlin with me as the Russians were about to enter the city. In the crowd of refugees, we got separated somehow. Mother had told me that if I got lost, I should head for the countryside because the kind farmers there would take me in. So that's what I did.

11-15

◇ straw (n.) 稻草
◇ out cold (adj.)（俚）不省人事
◇ flank (v.) 位於……的側面

◇ refugee (n.) 逃離者；難民

老夫婦立刻告訴我，我可以留下來，他們有三個兒子，兩個都已經打死了，一個仍在波蘭，前些日子仍有信來。他們好像很喜歡我，替我弄了一些熱的東西吃，吃了以後替我洗了澡，然後叫我再上床去睡覺。我放心了，也默默地告訴媽媽，希望她也能放心。

老夫婦年紀都相當大了，田裡的粗工都不能做，可是仍在田裡種些菜，我也幫他們的忙。他們都信仰基督教，主日一定會去教堂，我也跟著去，老夫婦告訴我，我媽媽塞進我衣物的一張紙，是我的領洗證明，這又令我困惑了，媽媽雖然常常去教堂，卻不帶我去，理由是我太小。可是我同年紀的朋友們卻都常進教堂，我知道媽媽會祈禱，可是從來不教我祈禱，現在要我離開家，為什麼要讓我知道其實我已經領洗，我領洗這件事顯然是個祕密。

有一天，我和老先生一起在田裡工作，忽然聽到附近教堂裡傳出鐘聲，老先生立刻停下工作，他告訴我歐戰一定已經結束了，我們全家人都到教堂慶祝，整個村莊的人都來了，我發現連一個年輕的男人都沒有出現，顯然我們國家將年輕男人幾乎都徵召去作戰了。

◇ hesitation (n.) 躊躇；猶豫
◇ combat (n.) 戰鬥
◇ advance (v.) 前進

◇ baptismal (adj.) 浸禮的；受禮的
◇ certificate (n.) 證書（動詞形態為 certify）

Without hesitation the couple told me that I could stay. They had three sons, two of whom had been killed in combat. The third was in Poland. They had received a letter from him a few days earlier. They appeared to take quite a liking to me: they fixed me a hot meal, and when I had eaten that, they gave me a bath. Then they told me to go back to bed for some rest. I felt safe, and I silently told my mother and hoped she felt sufe too.

The couple were fairly well advanced in years. Though no longer able to do hard work in the fields, they still planted vegetables, and I lent them a hand. Being Protestants, they attended church every Sunday, and I went along with them. The paper my mom had stuffed into my pocket was my baptismal certificate, they said. That left me puzzled—Mother had attended church often, but she never took me with her because I was too young. Yet all the other kids my age went to church. I knew my mother prayed, but she'd never taught me to pray. Why did she want me to know I'd been baptized now that I'd left home? Obviously my baptism had been a secret.

While I was working with the old man in the fields one day, I suddenly heard the local chapel's bells ringing. The old man stopped working immediately and told me that the war in Europe must be over. Our family went to the chapel together to celebrate; everyone in the village was there. I didn't see a single young man, though— evidently the country had conscripted nearly all of them into the army for the war.

◇ puzzled (adj.) 困惑
◇ chapel (n.) 教堂

◇ evidently (adv.) 顯然；明顯地
◇ conscript (v.) 徵召

到這時候，我已經叫他們爸爸媽媽，他們正式到法院登記收養了我，我也就有了養父養母。我的養父養母最大的願望就是要看到我在波蘭的二哥安全歸來。

16-20 　二哥終於回來了，我永遠記得他出現在家門口引起的興奮，養母抱著他又哭又笑。他問我的來歷以後，對我非常和氣。養母立刻到廚房裡張羅吃的東西，雖然不是什麼山珍海味，我的二哥仍將菜吃得一滴不剩，他說他這兩年來，每天都想吃媽媽做的菜。

　二哥安定下來以後，開始告訴我們納粹黨徒在波蘭殺害猶太人的罪行，二哥談這件事時，養父有時叫我離開，大概因為我是小孩子，不應該聽這些殘忍的事情。可是我仍知道了我們德國人如何制度化地殺害了無數的猶太人。

　有一天，二哥告訴我，有一個猶太小孩被抓去洗澡，他知道這就是他要被毒氣殺害的意思，這個小孩子講德國話，他問：「我是個小孩，我沒有犯了什麼錯，為什麼我要死？」說到這裡，二哥非常難

◇ adoption (n.) 收養
◇ officially (adv.) 官方地
◇ foster parent (n.) 養父母
◇ unharmed (adj.) 沒有受傷的；無恙的
◇ bring about (v.) 引起；促成

◇ embrace (v.) 擁抱（這個詞比hug正式，而且感覺更親密）
◇ weep (v.) 流淚
◇ rejoice (v.) 欣喜
◇ culinary (adj.) 烹飪的

At this point I was already calling them Father and Mother. They formally registered my adoption with the court, officially becoming my foster parents. Their greatest hope was to see my brother return from Poland unharmed.

At last, my brother came back. I'll always remember the excitement that his appearance on our doorstep brought about. Mother embraced him, weeping and rejoicing at the same time. Once he learned my story, he was very friendly to me. Mother promptly went to the kitchen to prepare a meal. It was no culinary masterpiece, but my brother ate every last bit of it. He had been craving Mother's cooking for two years, he said.

16-20

After my brother got settled, he began telling us about the atrocities the Nazis had perpetrated against the Jews in Poland. When he spoke of these things, Father sometimes asked me to leave the room probably because I was too young to hear about such brutality. But I still learned how we Germans systematically exterminated innumerable Jews.

One day my brother told me about a Jewish boy who was taken away for a "shower." Knowing that this meant he was going to be gassed to death, the German-speaking boy cried out, "I'm just a boy! I haven't done anything wrong. Why do I have to die?" Here my

---

⬦ crave（v.）非常想要
⬦ settle（v.）穩定下來（後面常加 down 或 in）
⬦ atrocity（n.）殘暴的行為

⬦ perpetrate（v.）犯（罪）（正式用語）
⬦ brutality（n.）殘忍；野蠻
⬦ exterminate（v.）殲滅

過，眼淚流了出來，我覺得他認為犯了一個很大的罪，因為他曾被迫
參加了這個慘無人道的大屠殺。

　　二哥對我影響至甚，我從此痛恨納粹黨人在第二次大戰的罪行，
也對於各種族、各宗教之間的隔閡非常不以為然。二哥改信天主教，
而且一不作，二不休，進入了山上的一座隱修院，以苦修來度其一
生。隱修士不僅不吃肉，也不互相講話，而且是永遠不離開隱修院
的，我們全家都參加了他入會的儀式。在葛雷果聖歌中，二哥穿了白
色的修士衣服走了出來，由於他的帽子幾乎遮住了他的臉，我差一點
兒認不出他來，我那時候只有九歲。二哥是我們家唯一能種田的人，
但養父母仍然一直鼓勵他去度這苦修的生活，他們知道二哥深深認為
人類罪孽深重，而要以苦修來替世人贖罪。

　　而我呢？我進了小學，而且表現很好，功課永遠第一名，我似乎也
有一些領導才能，因此我組織了一個學生社團，宗旨是促進不同種族
和不同宗教間的信任與諒解。我們發現附近有回教徒，就去參加他們

◇ break off (v.) 中斷
◇ overwhelm (v.) 壓倒；使……承受不了
◇ guilt (n.) 罪惡感
◇ compel (v.) 逼；強迫
◇ unconscionable (adj.) 沒良心的
◇ massacre (n.) 大屠殺

◇ oppose (v.) 反對
◇ conflict (n.) 衝突
◇ monastery (n.)(男生住的)修道院
◇ ascetic (adj.) 禁慾的
◇ penance (n.) 補贖；有贖罪作用的處罰

brother broke off, so upset that he wept. I think he was overwhelmed
with a terrible weight of guilt for being compelled to take part in such
an unconscionable massacre.

My brother had a great influence on me. Ever since then, I have
bitterly hated the Nazis and their war crimes, and I strongly oppose all
forms of conflict between races and religions. My brother converted
to Catholicism and entered a monastery in the mountains to spend
the rest of his days in ascetic penance. There, the monks not only
abstain from eating meat, but do not even speak to one another, and
they never leave the monastery. Our family attended his induction
ceremony together. Dressed in white monk's robes, my brother came
out amidst the sound of Gregorian chant. His hood almost completely
covered his face; I hardly recognized him. I was only nine years
old then. My brother was the only member of our family who could
plant our fields, but my parents still urged him to pursue his life of
penance. They knew my brother was convinced that humanity bore a
grievous burden of sin, and he intended to atone for that sin through
his suffering.

As for me, I went back to elementary school. I was a fine student,
always first in my class. I seemed to have some leadership ability
too, so I organized a student group to promote trust and understanding
among different races and religions. When we learned that there were

⬧ monk (n.) 修士 (和尚也叫monk)
⬧ abstain from (v.) 戒絕
⬧ amidst (prep.) 在……之中 (亦作amid)
⬧ hood (n.) 兜帽
⬧ grievous (adj.) 很嚴重；令人難過的
⬧ burden (n.) 負擔
⬧ atone (v.) 贖罪

的禮拜，我們多數是基督徒，可是一再邀請猶太教的教士來演講，也參加了他們的儀式。我希望當年納粹黨徒所傳播的種族仇恨再也不能發生了。

21-25　　我一直掛記著我的生母，我的老家劃入了東柏林，我花了很大的功夫，在我二十歲的那一年，進入了東柏林，發現我的老家已經不在了，當局造了一棟新的公寓，虧得我找到了一家雜貨店，雜貨店的老闆記得我媽媽。柏林陷落以後，我媽媽仍然活著，後來就搬走了。我有點悵然，可是知道媽媽沒死於砲火，也放心不少。

　　由於我的成績好，輕而易舉地得到獎學金，進入了哥廷根大學唸生物系，我有全額獎學金，可惜我養父在我大一的時候就去世了。畢業以後，我回到了鄉下，在一所中學教生物，也結了婚，有一個小女兒，養母和我們一起住。

　　我太太和我有同樣的觀點，我們都有宗教信仰，也推行不同種族之間的共融。

　　有一天晚上我在看電視，電視上有一個尋人節目，我偶爾會看這種節目，因為我希望看到我媽媽找我的消息，這一天，我竟然看到了，

◇ worship service (n.) 禮拜(通常用複數)　　　　◇ rabbi (n.) 猶太教祭司
◇ sow (v.) 播(種子)

Muslims in the neighborhood, we attended their worship services.
Most of us were Christians, but we often invited Jewish rabbis to
speak, and we took part in their services as well. I hoped that the
racial hatred the Nazis had sowed would never take root again.

I always wondered what happened to my birth mother. Our old
house had become part of East Berlin. After a great deal of effort,
I finally managed to travel to East Berlin the year I turned 20. Our
house was gone. In its place was a new government-built apartment.
Fortunately, I found a grocery store where the owner knew my
mother. She told me that Mother was still alive when Berlin fell, but
she had moved away since then. I was rather crestfallen, but it was
nice to know that she hadn't been killed in the war.

21-25

With my good grades, I easily won a full scholarship to study
biology at the University of Göttingen. Unfortunately, my adoptive
father died while I was a freshman. After I graduated, I moved
back to the countryside to work as a middle school biology teacher.
Somewhere along the way, I got married and had a daughter. My
adoptive mother lived together with us.

My wife and I are two of a kind. Both of us are religious, and we
try to promote interracial tolerance.

One night while I was watching TV, a people-search program
came on. I would occasionally watch this sort of program in the
hope of seeing news that my mother was looking for me. On this

◇ crestfallen (adj.) 氣餒的   ◇ tolerance (n.) 包容

雖然我媽媽老了很多，我仍然認得出她來，而且她的名字也完全正確。她已病重說她要跟我見最後一面。

我立刻趕去，當時我已二十八歲，離開她時，我只有八歲，媽媽當然認不出我來。可是我帶了十字架項鍊，也帶了領洗證明，我也可以說出許多小時候有趣的故事，媽媽知道她終於找到她的兒子。

26-30　　我告訴媽媽這二十年的經過，媽媽在病榻之上仔細地聽，可是她似乎最關心的是我對納粹黨的看法，我告訴她，我痛恨納粹的行為。她問我有無宗教信仰，我告訴她我們全家都信教，女兒一生出來就領了洗，每主日都去做禮拜。

媽媽最後問我一句話：「孩子，你是不是一個好人？」我告訴媽媽，我雖然不是聖人，但總應該是個好人。媽媽聽了以後，滿臉寬慰的表情，她說：「孩子，我放心了，我可以安心地走了，因為我的祈禱終於應驗了。」

我是一頭霧水，我不懂為什麼媽媽當年要拋棄我，現在又一再地

◇ considerably (adv.) 相當地
◇ relate (v.) 敘述
◇ amusing (adj.) 詼諧的；有趣的
◇ abhor (v.) 痛恨

particular night, I actually succeeded! Although my mother had
aged considerably, I could still recognize her, and the name she gave
matched perfectly. She was very ill, and she wanted to see me one
last time.

I went to her right away. I was 28 years old, but I had been only
eight when I left her, so of course she didn't recognize me at first. But
I brought my crucifix and baptismal certificate, and I related several
amusing incidents from my childhood. Mother knew she had found
her son at last.

I told her all that had happened to me over those twenty years, and
she listened intently from her hospital bed. But what she seemed to
care about the most was what I thought of the Nazis. I told her that I
abhorred what they had done. When she asked me if I was religious,
I told her that my family and I were all Christians: we baptized my
daughter as soon as she was born, and we went to church every
Sunday.

26-30

Finally, Mother asked me, "Son, are you a good man?" I told her
that although I was no saint, it was probably safe to say that I was
a good person. At this, a look of relief passed over her face. "Son,
now I can die in peace," she said. "My prayers have finally been
answered."

This left me utterly bewildered. I didn't understand why she
had abandoned me twenty years ago but was now so anxious about

◇ saint (n.) 聖徒　　　　　　◇ abandon (v.) 遺棄

關心我是不是一個好人。我就直截了當地問她，為什麼當年要我離開家？

媽媽叫我坐下，她說她要告訴我一個大的祕密，她說：「我不是你的媽媽，你的爸爸也不是你的爸爸。」

我當然大吃一驚，可是我看過我的領洗證明，領洗證明上清清楚楚地註明我的父母是誰。連出生的醫院都註明了，這到底是怎麼一回事呢？我問媽媽：「我明明是妳生的，怎麼說不是我的媽媽？那我的父母是誰？」

31-35　媽媽的回答更使我吃驚了，她說：「你沒有父母，你是複製的。」

我的心都要跳出來了，我學過生物，知道青蛙可以複製，高等動物的複製，我從未聽過。我問：「我是從誰的細胞複製成的？」

媽媽叫我心理上必須有所準備，因為事實真相會使我很難接受，媽媽告訴我，我是由希特勒的細胞複製而成的，從生物的觀點來看，我是另一個希特勒。

◇ point-blank (adv.) 直截了當地
◇ throw sb. for a loop (v.) 使……(某人)非常訝異

◇ protest (v..) 抗議；反對
◇ clone (n.) 複製人；複製品
◇ practically (adv.) 幾乎

whether I was a good man. I asked her point-blank: why had she made me leave home?

Then Mother sat me down and said she had a gigantic secret to tell me. "I'm not your mother," she said, "and your father wasn't your father."

Naturally, that threw me for a loop. But I'd seen my baptismal certificate, and my parents' names were written there, clear as could be. Even the name of the hospital where I was born was recorded. How could what she had said be true? "Of course I'm your son!" I protested. "What do you mean you're not my mother? Then who are my parents?"

Her answer to that really threw me for a loop. "You have no parents," she said. "You're a clone."

My heart practically jumped out of my chest. Having studied biology, I knew that frogs could be cloned, but I'd never heard of the cloning of higher-order animals. "Whose cells was I cloned from?" I asked.

Mother told me to prepare myself for the answer, because I wasn't going to like it at all. She told me that I had been cloned from the cells of Adolf Hitler. From a biological point of view, I was a second Hitler.

31-35

◇ order (n.) 等級　　　　　◇ cell (n.) 細胞

　　媽媽告訴我，在發動第二次世界大戰以前，希特勒就想複製他自己，他知道哥廷根大學的勒狄維克教授曾經複製過青蛙，因此強迫勒狄維克教授複製一個希特勒，否則會對他家人不利，勒狄維克教授不敢不從，卻果真成功了。當然他們需要一個女性來懷這個胎兒，希特勒找到了我的爸爸媽媽，大概是我的爸爸媽媽非常單純，跟政治毫無關連，媽媽身體也健康，因此我的媽媽被迫懷了我。

　　希特勒常常派人來看我成長，他下令我絕對不可以有任何宗教信仰，這就是媽媽不敢帶我上教堂的原因，可是我的爸媽以極快又極祕密的方式替我領了洗。在我爸爸最後一次上前線以前，他拜託媽媽一件事，那就是一定要將我變成一個好人，好讓希特勒的心願不能得逞。

36-40　　我們家門口一直有一個兵在監視我們，當媽媽發現那個兵撤退以後，她知道我必須逃離納粹的監視。因為希特勒失敗了，可是那些死忠的納粹黨徒很可能認為我是他們唯一的希望，這樣，我的命運就悲慘了。她更怕蘇聯軍隊已知道了我的存在，所以她決定將我趕出家門，她有信心我會被好心的農人家庭收容，我也會在好的環境中成長。我離開了以後，媽媽說每天晚上祈禱中都不曾忘過我，她本來

◇ obey (v.) 服從
◇ bear (v.) 生(小孩)
◇ presumably (adv.) 據推測；大概
◇ hasty (adj.) 匆匆的；倉促的

According to my mother, before starting World War II, Hitler had wanted to clone himself. He knew there was a Professor Ludwig at Göttingen University who had cloned frogs, so he went to him and told the professor that he had better make a Hitler clone or something unfortunate would happen to his family. Terrified, Professor Ludwig obeyed; to his surprise, the process succeeded. Of course, Hitler needed a woman to bear the child. So he chose my father and mother, presumably because they were simple people who had nothing to do with politics, and Mother had a healthy body. Thus she was forced to become pregnant with me.

As I grew up, Hitler often sent men to watch me. He ordered that under no circumstances was I to belong to any religion—that was why my mother had never dared to take me to church. But my parents did manage to baptize me in a hasty secret ceremony. Before my father went to the front line for the last time, he made my mother promise to raise me to be a good man so that Hitler's plans for me would be thwarted.

There had always been a sentry posted by our door to keep a watchful eye on me. When Mother saw the sentry leave, she knew I had to escape from the surveillance of the Nazis—otherwise, when Hitler was defeated, his faithful Nazi followers would see me as their only hope, and I would meet a miserable fate. At the same time, she feared that the Soviet troops might learn of my existence. So

36-40

◇ thwart (v.) 使……挫敗
◇ sentry (n.) 哨兵
◇ post (v.) 站崗；布置(崗哨)

◇ surveillance (n.) 監視
◇ defeat (v.) 打敗
◇ troop (n.) 軍隊；部隊 (通常用複數)

搬到一個小鎮去住，後來他開始和老朋友聯絡，大家也都問起我，可是好像沒有一個人知道我的來歷，她放心了，因為當初知道我來歷的人本來就不多，現在這些人一定都已經死掉了。所以她決定再和我聯絡。

媽媽說她可以安心地走了，因為她要在天堂裡告訴我爸爸，我是一個好人，這是爸爸最大的願望。

媽媽告訴我這個故事以後，顯得很疲憊，醫生告訴我，媽媽病重，唯一記掛的就是我，現在她看到了我，大概就不會活多久了。他叫我不要離開，果真媽媽不久就進入彌留狀態了，大概兩個小時以後，媽媽忽然醒了，她叫我靠近她，用很微弱的聲音對我說：「孩子，千萬不要留小鬍子。」說完以後，媽媽笑得好可愛，像一個小孩子一樣，幾分鐘後，媽媽去世了。

我將媽媽安葬以後，到哥廷根大學去找勒狄維克教授，其實我曾經上過他的課，這位教授看到我，一副非常愧疚的表情，他說他的確複製了希特勒，可是完全出於被逼。他知道我的生活和想法以後，陷入於沉思之中，他說我絕不是希特勒想要製造的分身。

◇ concern (n.) 擔心；掛念
◇ drift (v.) 飄流 （drift into 漸漸陷入）
◇ unconsciousness (n.) 無意識的狀態
◇ observe (v.) 說出(觀察或思考的結果)
◇ twisted (adj.) 古怪的；變態的
◇ conquer (v.) 征服

she decided to make me leave home, trusting that some kindhearted farming family out there would take me in and give me a good environment to grow up in. Mother said that since the day I left, she had never once forgotten me in her nightly prayers. She moved to a small town and gradually began contacting her old friends. They all asked about me, but none of them seemed to know my secret. She stopped worrying—very few people had known to begin with, and they were surely dead by now. So she decided to contact me.

Mother said that she could die in peace, for now she would be able to tell my father in heaven that I was a good man. That had been his greatest wish.

After she finished her story, Mother looked exhausted. The doctor told me that all through her illness, her only concern had been for me, and now that she had seen me, she probably wouldn't live much longer. He asked me not to leave. Sure enough, she soon drifted into unconsciousness. About two hours later, she suddenly awoke. She called me over and said in a very faint voice, "Son, no matter what happens, don't ever grow a mustache." Then she smiled charmingly, like a child. A few minutes later, she passed away.

After she had been laid to rest, I went to Göttingen University to see Professor Ludwig. I had actually taken classes from him in the past. When the professor saw me, a look of guilt and shame appeared on his face. He told me it was true that he had cloned Hitler, but only because he had been forced to. When he learned of my life and beliefs, he fell deep into thought. I was definitely not the clone Hitler

　　勒狄維克教授告訴我，他知道希特勒是不能複製另一個希特勒的。希特勒之所以是希特勒，主要是他有特殊的想法，他恨猶太人，他要征服全世界，也想讓純種的亞利安民族統治全世界，這種瘋狂的想法，並不能由一個單細胞所移植。

41-44　　勒狄維克教授還告訴我一個驚人的祕密，他仍然保有希特勒的細胞，他問我要不要由他做一個實驗，以證明我的DNA和希特勒的DNA是完全一樣的。

　　我拒絕了，我不要人家檢查我的DNA是不是希特勒的DNA，我不是希特勒，我是我。希特勒心中充滿仇恨，我從來沒有。希特勒有極為病態的種族偏見，我卻一直致力於不同種族之間的諒解。

　　希特勒想要複製一個他自己，他當然想控制我，他錯了，他甚至不能控制他自己的命運，如何能控制我的命運？

　　在開車回家的路上，收音機播出葛雷果聖歌動人的音樂，我想起了在隱修院的二哥。我忽然了解了，我和希特勒最大的不同，恐怕是我有這個肯替世人犧牲一切的二哥，而希特勒沒有這個福分。

◇ insane (adj.) 瘋狂的
◇ notion (n.) 想法；主意
◇ transplant (v.) 移植
◇ startling (adj.) 驚人的

◇ confirm (v.) 證明
◇ inspect (v.) 檢查
◇ pathological (adj.) 病態的
◇ racist (n.) 種族歧視者

had hoped for, he observed.

Professor Ludwig had known all along that Hitler couldn't make another Hitler. What made Hitler Hitler was mainly his twisted ideas: he hated Jews, he wanted to conquer the world, and he wanted the pure Aryan race to rule the earth. Insane notions like that couldn't be transplanted in a cell.

41-44

Professor Ludwig went on to tell me a startling secret: he still had some of Hitler's cells. He asked me whether I would like him to confirm by experiment that my DNA was the same as Hitler's.

I said no. I didn't want anyone inspecting my DNA to see if it was the same as Hitler's. I'm not Hitler—I'm me. Hitler's heart was full of hate, but mine has never been. Hitler was a pathological racist, but I've always promoted interracial understanding.

Naturally, by cloning himself, Hitler intended to control me. He was wrong. He couldn't even control his own fate—how could he control mine?

As I drove home, a lovely Gregorian chant played on the radio. I thought of my brother in the monastery. Then suddenly it came to me. The greatest difference between me and Hitler was that I had a brother willing to sacrifice everything for his fellow man, but Hitler never had such a blessing.

◇ intend (v.) 意圖
◇ willing (adj.) 願意的
◇ fellow man (n.) 人類同胞

(1) hardly 根本不(1 段)

Our situation was hardly unusual—nearly all my neighborhood friends had lost their fathers in the war too.

這不是什麼了不起的事，我的鄰居玩伴們，幾乎都失去了爸爸。

【解析】

副詞 hardly 修飾動詞，意為「幾乎不」，例如：We hardly know each other. (我們幾乎不認識。)；也能用 hardly 來表示「才剛……」，例如：We had hardly started our trip when our car broke down.(我們才剛開始旅行，車子就拋錨了。)

然而 hardly 在故事中卻作「根本不，一點也不」解釋，帶有一點諷刺的意味，例如：She hardly looked happy to see me.(她看到我，臉色看起來一點也不高興。)

【小試身手】

1-1. 我們幾乎沒有時間說再見。

_____

1-2. 你是辛苦工作呢，還是幾乎沒有在工作？(原為美國的老笑話)

_____

1-3. 他根本不是我們最出色的員工。

_____

（2）once 曾有一時

　　grow emptier and emptier 變得越來越少（2 段）

Stores that were once well stocked with goods grew emptier and emptier.

本來店裡可以買到很多的東西，現在東西越來越少。

解析

句子中的 once 可譯為「曾有一時」，而視上下文也能譯為「曾有一次」，是用來比較過去與現在的好用字。例如：Once a popular tourist destination, the town has fallen on hard times.（這個小鎮曾為人氣觀光景點，但已經歷了一段難熬的日子。）

once 常用來表達對過去的緬懷，這也是童話故事為什麼大多以 Once upon a time...（很久很久以前）來開頭。

此外，另一個須注意的重點是如何翻譯「變得越來越……」，句中的 grew 等同於 became，而「形容詞比較級 and 形容詞比較級」指「越來越……」，故 emptier and emptier 則指「越來越少」。

小試身手

2-1. 哇，你長得越來越高呢！

_____

2-2. 最近我越來越少看到她。

_____

2-3. 我也曾經年輕美麗過啊。

_____

(3) a ___ of a ___ 表達情緒
　　 run short of（run low, run out, etc.）（3 段）

Our neighbors envied us—they had a devil of a time trying to buy milk and meat, but my mother and I never ran short of either.

鄰居都羨慕我們，他們很難買到牛奶和肉，我和我母親卻從不缺乏牛奶和肉。

解析

你可能知道 devil 意指魔鬼，但你可能不知道 devil 也可當感嘆詞用，表示驚訝，可譯為「才怪」，而 devil 還可單純用來加強語氣，意指「究竟、到底」，如：What the devil?（到底發生了什麼事？）。故事中的 a devil of a time 意為「非常艱困的時期」，因此上句可改寫為 They found it very difficult to buy milk and meat.，但是原句的寫法比較生動。

在非正式的美語中，「a ___ of a ___」是表達情緒的好用句。如果有機會到美國旅行，仔細聽聽美國人對話，你就會聽到類似這樣的說法：

◇ 他是個很棒的男人。
　 He's a heck of a guy.＝He's a great guy.

◇ 嗯，今天真難熬。
　 Well, it's been a hell of a day.＝It's been a very long, difficult, or otherwise remarkable day.

◇ 這真是一部爛片。
　 It was a real dog of a movie.＝It was a lousy movie.

接著是一個看起來有點怪的片語 run short of，意思是「你常用而且應該份量足夠的某樣東西快用完了」，類似的片語為 run out 和 run low。切記，這些片語一定要熟記，因為如果你在英語系國家開車開到一半沒油了（run out of gas），就派得上用場了。

最後須注意的是，run short of something 表示「不夠用」，而 run low 則指「份量還夠，但很快就得要再補充了」，英文看起來差不多，但真正的意思卻不一樣。

小試身手

3-1. 我的氧氣快用完了，所以我回到水面。

_____

3-2. 我無法做餅乾，因為我們的麵粉不夠用。

_____

3-3. 你最好不要再做那件事，我快沒耐心了。

_____

（4）remain 保持、仍然（4 段）

But I remained skeptical of my mother's explanation.
我可不太相信媽媽的話。

解析

如果有句英文你聽不懂，請美國朋友解釋了以後，還是不懂，在那樣的情況下，就可以說：Even after hearing my friend's explanation, I remained confused. (就算聽了我朋友的解釋，我還是不懂。) 在這種情況下，remain 意指「仍是」，但 remain 也可指「保持、維持(某種狀態)」，如 remain standing (繼續站著)和 remain calm in an emergency(在緊急狀態中保持冷靜)。

小試身手

4-1. 雖然她向他道歉，他依然不高興。

＿＿＿＿＿＿＿＿＿＿＿＿＿＿＿＿＿＿＿＿＿＿＿＿＿

4-2. 我們整夜留在阿公的身邊。

＿＿＿＿＿＿＿＿＿＿＿＿＿＿＿＿＿＿＿＿＿＿＿＿＿

5.　by the [unit] 以〔單位〕計算（6 段）

The shelling came nearer, and Mother grew more anxious by the day.

砲聲聽起來越來越近，媽媽也越來越焦慮。

解析

你的公司怎麼計算你的薪資呢？工作大致可分為時薪(pay by the hour)、日薪(by the day)、月薪(by the month)和年薪制(by the year)。也有些工作是以工作量來計算，如翻譯通常是以字數來計算，而「by the＋單位」就是「以(單位)計算」。現在你應該推敲得出 grew more nervous by the day 的意思了，其中的 by the day 意為「以天來算」或「日益」，故整句可翻為「日益焦慮」或「一天比一天焦慮」。

小試身手

5-1. (天氣)一天比一天寒冷。

＿＿＿＿＿＿＿＿＿＿＿＿＿＿＿＿＿＿＿＿＿＿＿＿＿

5-2. 7-Eleven的員工領時薪；工程師領月薪。

＿＿＿＿＿＿＿＿＿＿＿＿＿＿＿＿＿＿＿＿＿＿＿＿＿

（6）the sooner the better 越快越好（8 段）

Flee Berlin immediately, the sooner the better.
趕快逃離柏林，越快越好。

解析

我們之前學過「越來越……」的說法，現在我們要來學學怎麼說「越 A 越 B」。也許有人看到「越快越好」就會翻成 the faster the better，不過道地慣用語為 the sooner the better，因為在很多情況下都適用，soon 可指「立刻」、「快」和「早」，例如：

◇ 醫生，我們需要你立刻到醫院來，越快越好。
   Doctor, we need you at the hospital right away. The sooner you can be here the better.

◇ 草莓越熟，味道越甜。
   The riper the strawberry, the sweeter the taste.

┌───┐
│ 小試身手 │
│ │
│ 6-1. 你當然可以邀請朋友來！人越多越好玩。 │
│ │
│ ＿＿＿＿＿＿＿＿＿＿＿＿＿＿＿＿＿＿＿＿＿＿＿ │
│ │
│ 6-2. 他跑得越快，贏的機率就越高。 │
│ │
│ ＿＿＿＿＿＿＿＿＿＿＿＿＿＿＿＿＿＿＿＿＿＿＿ │
│ │
└───┘

（7）be to... 要……（用於發號施令或給予指示）（8 段）

Once I got there, I was to find a family who would take me in.
到了鄉下，我應該設法讓一個家庭收容我。

解析

這可能是你不太熟悉的命令句型，通常是上位者在對下位者發號施令或給予指示時使用，例如：

◇ 當史密斯先生的郵件送來時，你要拿去他的辦公室。
When Mr. Smith's mail arrives, you are to carry it to his office.

◇ 無論如何你都不准開我的車。
You are not under any circumstances to drive my car.

看了以上例句，你應該能體會那種上對下的感覺，這種命令句不太會出現在現在美式口語中，但可以在文章中發現。

小試身手

7. 父親說我不可以玩他的工具。

_____

(8) in one's mind's eye　在想像中（9 段）

In my mind's eye, I could see their tanks rolling in.
我可以想像得到俄國坦克進城的景象。

解析

人睡覺時眼睛是閉著的，但是你還是可以運用想像力「看」到東西。莎士比亞的經典之作《哈姆雷特》就發明了 in one's mind's eye 這個片語來形容這個能力。

◇ 哈姆雷特：我想我看到了我父親。
Hamlet: Methinks I see my father.
賀瑞修：在哪裡看到的，王上？
Horatio: Where, my lord?
哈姆雷特：賀瑞修，在想像中看到的。
Hamlet: In my mind's eye, Horatio.

哈姆雷特的父親過世了，但哈姆雷特還是能在想像中看到他。同樣地，故事中的主述者離城市很遠，但他還是能想像出一大堆蘇聯坦克進城的景象。我們如果用想像，往往可以看到肉眼所看不到的東西。

小試身手

8. 我們已經下山了，但是阿里山燦爛的日出依然留在我想像中。

_____

(9) find oneself... 發現自己(處在一個不知道如何到達的環境或情況)(11 段)

When I awoke, I found myself lying in a comfortable bed.
醒來以後，我發現我躺在一張舒適的床上。

解析

我讀大學時有一次騎著單車去上學，另一輛單車突然出現，為了避免發生車禍，我死命煞車，整個人飛過車頭，頭著地跌了個狗吃屎。在我恢復意識後，我發現自己平躺在地上(I found myself lying flat on my back)，看著一堆不認識的人在問我是否安好。送醫後，醫生跟我說我有輕微的腦震盪。自從發生那次意外之後，我騎車總是會戴安全帽。

我用這個例子來解釋 find oneself somewhere 就是指「某人不太清楚自己為什麼和如何到達某地或處於某種狀態」。閣下曾發生過類似的事嗎？

小試身手

9. 海倫參加了電視上的音樂比賽，做夢也沒想到自己會贏。突然間她發現自己名利雙收，感覺很奇怪。

_____

（10）take a liking to... 喜歡上……（12 段）

They appeared to take quite a liking to me.

他們好像很喜歡我。

解析

take a liking to someone 意為「第一次見到某人時，就喜歡上那人」，是比較口語的說法。記得你第一次去見你另一半的父母親嗎？你可能很擔心他們對你有沒有好印象，幸運的話，他們會喜歡你，但他們也有可能拿著球棒，追你追出家門。

須注意 take a liking to 不是情侶或夫妻之間的「喜歡」，而是朋友、同事、同學之間的「喜歡」。

小試身手

10. 新來的會計師有很強的工作能力，老闆一看就喜歡。

_____

（11）lend a hand 幫個忙（13 段）

Though no longer able to do hard work in the fields, they still planted vegetables, and I lent them a hand.

他們田裡的粗工都不能做，可是仍在田裡種些菜，我也幫他們的忙。

解析

中文的「幫手」可對應為英文中的一個片語 lend a hand，兩者唯一的差別在於「幫手」不能當動詞用，lend a hand 不能當名詞用，但是基本意涵是一樣的，只須把「幫手」改成「幫個忙」就很容易了解。

11. 我抬不動這個書桌，你能不能來幫個忙？

_____

(12) convert to（a religion）改信（某個宗教）（19 段）

My brother converted to Catholicism.

二哥改信天主教。

解析

convert 意為「改變、轉換」，例如：They converted the old house into a museum.（他們把老房子改建成博物館。）這個字也常用在兌換貨幣上，例如：I'd like to convert my Taiwan dollars into euros, please.（我想把台幣換成歐元，麻煩您。）在故事中的 convert 則是指放棄原本的信仰而轉而皈依另一種宗教，主述者的哥哥原本是新教徒（Protestant），但他選擇變成天主教徒（Catholic）。有一點要特別注意，atheist（無神論者）可以 convert to（改信）某種宗教，但一個原本就有宗教信仰的人變成無神論者不能用 convert 這個字。此外，convert 也可以當及物動詞使用，例如：She was converted by Christian missionaries.（她因基督教傳教士改變信仰。）convert 也可當名詞用（注意，名詞的發音不一樣喔），所以前面那個例句可以改寫為：She is a convert to Christianity.（她改信基督教。）

12-1. 你知不知道怎麼把公斤換算成磅？

_____

12-2. 他生來就是猶太人，可是他太太是後來改信猶太教的。

_____

（13）somewhere along the way 過去某段時間（22 段）

Somewhere along the way, I got married and had a daughter.

我也結了婚，有一個小女兒。

解析

句中的 the way 是指「人生已經走過的路」，而介系詞 along 意為「沿著、順著」，所以 somewhere along the way 可用以比喻 at some time in the past，表「過去某個時間」。

當然，along the way 或 on the way 也可以單就字面上的意思來用，如：

◇ 我們半路停下來吃午餐。
  We stopped for lunch along the way.

◇ 往市區的路上有一家麥當勞。
  There's a McDonald's on the way to downtown.

◇ 我們回家前會順便去一下雜貨店。
  We'll stop by the grocery store on our way home.

小試身手

13. 比爾和我高中畢業二十年了。在這二十年間，我們失去了聯絡。

_____

（14）two of a kind 英雄所見略同（23 段）

My wife and I are two of a kind.

我太太和我有同樣的觀點。

解析

玩撲克牌時，如果你拿到兩張相同的牌，就叫做「一對」(a pair)，但如果有三張相同的牌就叫做三條(three of a kind)，如果夠幸運的話，你也有可能拿到鐵支(four of a kind)。不過，把人拿來做比較時，通常一次只比較兩個人，如果兩個人的個性非常相似，英文說法就是 two of a kind，不用 pair 來表示是怕別人會誤以為這兩人正在交往。

小試身手

14. 他們每次見面，談話內容淨是羽球。他們倆真是彼此的知音啊！

_____

（15）it is safe to say... 可以安全地說（27 段）

I told her that although I was no saint, it was probably safe to say that I was a good person.

我告訴媽媽，我雖不是聖人，但總應該算是個好人。

解析

從這句話可以明顯看出說話者想要委婉地表示自己是個好人，以免顯得自大。因此，他不是直接說 I am a good person.，而換了這種婉轉的說法："Most people would feel safe saying that I am a good person." 換句話說，他仰賴「別人」的意見來支持他自己所做的結論。那樣一來，即使他的結論到頭來是錯的，他也不會覺得尷尬。

此外，句型 It seems / looks＋adj. (that) ……一樣也可以表示客觀又婉轉的說法：

◇ 推斷詹森先生一點都沒錯似乎是合理的。
　 It seems reasonable to conclude that Mr. Jameson did nothing wrong.

小試身手

15-1. 背誦你不了解的詩好像有點蠢。

_____

15-2. 看起來洋基隊應該會贏這場球賽吧。

_____

(16) point-blank 直截了當(28 段)

I asked her point-blank: why had she made me leave home?

我就直截了當地問她,為什麼當年要我離開家?

解析

point-blank 起初是用來表示「近距離地用槍指著某樣東西,因此幾乎可以百分百命中目標」,而且 point-blank 可以作副詞或形容詞用,例如:

◇ 囚犯被告知說如果試圖逃獄的話他就會被就地正法。
The prisoner was told that if he tried to escape, he'd be shot point-blank.

◇ 那種槍不會打不中,尤其是直接射擊時。
A gun like that doesn't miss, especially at point-blank range.

你應該可以感受到此片語帶有「直接」的含意,所以 point-blank 用來表示「直截了當」或「直接」:

◇ 她直接告訴我以後都不想再見到我了。
She told me point-blank that she never wanted to see me again.

小試身手

16-1. 他直截了當的控訴令我十分訝異。

_____

16-2. 我向攻擊我的人直接開槍。

_____

17. (as) ___ as can be ……到了極點(30 段)

But I'd seen my baptismal certificate, and my parents' names were written there, clear as could be.

可是我看過我的領洗證明，領洗證明上清清楚楚地註明我的父母是誰。

解析

此片語的 be 意指 exist(存在的)。如要更加詳細地表達此片語，clear as could be 會變成 as clear as anything could possibly exist。(主述者用 could 代替 can，因為整句的時態是過去式。)換句話說即 nothing else could possibly be clearer。

記住，這個片語只是介系詞 as 表比較的一個例子，其他用法還有：

◇ 我像國王一樣快樂。
　 I'm as happy as a king.

◇ 夜黑如墨。
　 The night was black as ink.

如果你沒辦法想出另一個明確的東西來作比較，可以在第二個 as 後面加上一個子句：

◇ 我很久沒有這麼健康了。
　 I'm healthy as I've been in a long time.

17-1. 她和小孩一樣天真。

_____

17-2. 考試的結果讓我失望。（我考得不如我所希望的。）

_____

17-3. 我以為爬那座山會很辛苦，結果反而輕鬆得不得了。

_____

（18）had better..., or（else）... 你最好要……，不然會……（34 段）

So he went to him and told the professor that he had better make a Hitler clone or something unfortunate would happen to his family.

因此(他)強迫勒狄維克教授複製一個希特勒，否則會對他家人不利。

解析

中文裡的威脅詞大多是：「你最好……，否則你會……」，跟英文說法相當接近，「最好」就是 had better，而「否則」可以譯成 or else 或是更簡單的 or。我們可以用這個句型來表達措辭強烈的嚴重威脅，例如：

◇ 你最好把刀子放下，否則我就要開槍打你了。
   You had better put down that knife, or I'll shoot you.

當然也可用來表示小小的威脅：

◇ 你最好現在寫功課，不然一個禮拜都不准看電視。
   You'd better do your homework right now, or no TV for a week.

有時候也可以用 or else 作為結尾，讓被威脅的一方自行想像後果：

◇ 星期五以前把我的錢給我，否則的話，嘿嘿……！
Give me my money by Friday or else!

小試身手

18-1. 她說我最好不要再抄她的考卷，否則她會告訴老師。

_____

18-2. 離我家人遠一點！否則的話，嘿嘿……！

_____

19. have to do with... 跟……有關係(34 段)

So he chose my father and mother, presumably because they were
simple people who had nothing to do with politics.
希特勒找到了我的爸爸媽媽，大概是因為我的爸爸媽媽非常單純，跟政
治毫無關連。

解析

你跟朋友正在聊某件事時，他突然說了一個風馬牛不相及的事情，你就可
以問：What does that have to do with anything?(這跟我們的話題有什麼
關係？)又好比警察正在盤問嫌犯有關銀行搶案時，可能會聽到該名嫌犯
說：I had nothing to do with that. (我跟那個案子一點關係都沒有。)要注意
nothing 的位置一定放在 had 和 to do 之間，所以可以把 have nothing to do
當成一個完整片語來背。

小試身手

19-1. 我忘了她演講的內容，但是好像跟核能有關。

_____

19-2. 新聞學和數學有什麼關係？

_____

19-3. 研究顯示，工作表現和性別毫無關係。

_____

(20) all through; all along 一直（38 段／40 段）

The doctor told me that all through her illness, her only concern had been for me.

醫生告訴我，媽媽病重，唯一記掛的就是我。

Professor Ludwig had known all along that Hitler couldn't make another Hitler.

勒狄維克教授告訴我，他早就知道希特勒是不能複製另一個希特勒的。

解析

all through her illness 意指「在她生病的這一整段時間」，強調母親對子的關心，不論她病得多重，都還是會先想到他。同樣地，勒狄維克教授從複製希特勒的細胞那一天起，就知道希特勒的計畫不會成功。他一直（all along）都知道。

through 和 along 的差別在於，前者用來描述經過的事件（pass through），後者則是用來表示「沿著」，這樣就比較好懂了，例如：

◇ 我們談話談了一整夜。
We talked all through the night.

◇ 我一直都愛你。
I have loved you all along.

all along 也可以照字面上的意思解釋，有時 all 可以省略，例如：

◇ 沿路上都有燈。
There were lights all along the road.

◇ 我們開車慢慢穿過濃霧。
We drove slowly through the fog.

小試身手

20-1. 如果你一直都知道，你為什麼沒有告訴我？

_____

20-2. 那雪留在地上整個冬天都沒有融化。

_____

20-3. 我們沿著一條穿過森林的窄路開車。

_____

小試身手解答

1-1. We hardly had time to say goodbye.

1-2. Are you working hard or hardly working?

1-3. He's hardly our best worker.

2-1. Wow, you keep growing taller and taller!

2-2. Lately I've been seeing her less and less.

2-3. I was young and beautiful once.

3-1. I was running low on oxygen, so I returned to the surface.

3-2. I can't make cookies because we're running short of flour.

3-3. You'd better stop doing that—I'm running out of patience.

4-1. Even though she apologized to him, he remained upset.

4-2. We remained by Grandpa's side all through the night.

5-1. It's getting colder by the day.

5-2. 7-Eleven employees are paid by the hour; engineers are paid by the month.

6-1. Of course you can invite a friend! The more the merrier.

6-2. The faster he runs, the more likely he is to win.

7. Father said I was not to play with his tools.

8. We had climbed down from the mountain, but I could still see the glorious Alishan sunrise in my mind's eye.

9. Helen entered a music competition on TV, never dreaming that she would win. All of a sudden she found herself rich and famous—it felt very strange.

10. The new accountant was very good at his job; the boss took a liking to him immediately.

11. I can't lift this desk—could you lend me a hand?

12-1. Do you know how to convert kilograms to pounds?

12-2. He was born a Jew, but his wife is a convert to Judaism.

13. Twenty years have passed since Bill and I graduated from high school. Somewhere along the way, we lost touch with each other.

14. Whenever they're together, they talk about nothing but badminton. They sure are two of a kind!

15-1. It seems a little silly to memorize poems that you don't understand.

15-2. It looks safe to say that the Yankees are going to win this game.

16-1. His point-blank accusation surprised me.

16-2. I fired point-blank at my attacker.

17-1. She is as innocent as a child.

17-2. I didn't do as well on the test as I had hoped to.

17-3. I thought climbing the mountain would be difficult, but it was easy as could be.

18-1. She told me I had better not copy off her test again, or she'd tell the teacher.

18-2. Stay away from my family or else!

19-1. I forgot what her speech was about, but I think it had something to do with nuclear energy.

19-2. What does journalism have to do with math?

19-3. Studies have shown that work performance has nothing to do with gender.

20-1. If you knew all along, why didn't you tell me?

20-2. The snow stayed on the ground all through the winter.

20-3. We drove along a narrow road that went through a forest.

Linking English

讀李家同學英文6：李花村

2009年1月初版　　　　　　　　　　　　定價：新臺幣320元
2018年3月二版
有著作權・翻印必究
Printed in Taiwan.

著　　者	李	家	同	
譯　　者	Nick Hawkins			
解　　析	周	正	一	
	Nick Hawkins			
叢書主編	林	雅	玲	
校　　對	林	慧	如	
	曾	婷	姬	
	鄭	彥	谷	
封面設計	翁	國	鈞	
內文排版	陳	如	琪	

出　版　者　聯經出版事業股份有限公司　　總編輯　胡　金　倫
地　　　址　新北市汐止區大同路一段369號1樓　總經理　陳　芝　宇
編輯部地址　新北市汐止區大同路一段369號1樓　社　長　羅　國　俊
台北聯經書房　台北市新生南路三段94號　　發行人　林　載　爵
　　　電話　(0 2) 2 3 6 2 0 3 0 8
台中分公司　台中市北區崇德路一段198號
暨門市電話　(0 4) 2 2 3 1 2 0 2 3
郵政劃撥帳戶第0100559-3號
郵撥電話　(0 2) 2 3 6 2 0 3 0 8
印　刷　者　文聯彩色製版印刷有限公司
總　經　銷　聯合發行股份有限公司
發　行　所　新北市新店區寶橋路235巷6弄6號2F
　　　電話　(0 2) 2 9 1 7 8 0 2 2

行政院新聞局出版事業登記證局版臺業字第0130號

本書如有缺頁，破損，倒裝請寄回台北聯經書房更換。　　ISBN　978-957-08-5094-9 (平裝)
聯經網址 http://www.linkingbooks.com.tw
電子信箱 e-mail:linking@udngroup.com

國家圖書館出版品預行編目資料

讀李家同學英文6：李花村 / 李家同著 .
Nick Hawkins譯 . 周正一、Nick Hawkins解析 .
二版 . 新北市 . 聯經 . 2018.03
240面；14.8×21公分 . (Linking English)
　　ISBN　978-957-08-5094-9（平裝）
　　[2018年3月二版]

1.英語　2.讀本

805.18　　　　　　　　　　　　　107002750